THEODORE SAVAGE

THEODORE SAVAGE

Cicely Hamilton

introduction by Susan R. Grayzel

THE MIT PRESS
CAMBRIDGE, MASSACHUSETTS
LONDON, ENGLAND

This book was set in Arnhem Pro and PF DIN Text Pro by New Best-set Typesetters Ltd. Printed and bound in the United States of America.

Library of Congress Cataloging-in-Publication Data

Names: Hamilton, Cicely, 1872–1952, author. | Grayzel, Susan R., writer of introduction.
Title: Theodore Savage / Cicely Hamilton ; introduction by Susan R. Grayzel.
Description: Cambridge, Massachusetts : The MIT Press, [2023] | Series: Radium age
Identifiers: LCCN 2022014405 (print) | LCCN 2022014406 (ebook) | ISBN 9780262545228 (paperback) | ISBN 9780262373623 (epub) | ISBN 9780262373616 (pdf)
Subjects: LCGFT: Dystopian fiction. | Novels.
Classification: LCC PR6015.A44 T47 2023 (print) | LCC PR6015.A44 (ebook) | DDC 823/.912—dc23/eng/20220415
LC record available at https://lccn.loc.gov/2022014405
LC ebook record available at https://lccn.loc.gov/2022014406

10 9 8 7 6 5 4 3 2 1

CONTENTS

Joshua Glenn

Do we really know science fiction? There were the scientific romance years that stretched from the mid-nineteenth century to circa 1900. And there was the genre's so-called golden age, from circa 1935 through the early 1960s. But between those periods, and overshadowed by them, was an era that has bequeathed us such tropes as the robot (berserk or benevolent), the tyrannical superman, the dystopia, the unfathomable extraterrestrial, the sinister telepath, and the eco-catastrophe. A dozen years ago, writing for the sf blog io9.com at the invitation of Annalee Newitz and Charlie Jane Anders, I became fascinated with the period during which the sf genre as we know it emerged. Inspired by the exactly contemporaneous career of Marie Curie, who shared a Nobel Prize for her discovery of radium in 1903, only to die of radiation-induced leukemia in 1934, I eventually dubbed this three-decade interregnum the "Radium Age."

Curie's development of the theory of radioactivity, which led to the extraordinary, terrifying, awe-inspiring insight that the atom is, at least in part, a state of energy constantly in movement, is an apt metaphor for the twentieth century's first three decades. These years were marked by rising sociocultural strife across various fronts: the founding of the women's suffrage movement, the National Association for the Advancement of Colored People, socialist currents within the labor movement, anticolonial and revolutionary upheaval around the world . . . as well as the associated strengthening of reactionary movements that supported, for example, racial segregation, immigration restriction, eugenics, and sexist policies.

Science—as a system of knowledge, a mode of experimenting, and a method of reasoning—accelerated the pace of change during these years in ways simultaneously liberating and terrifying. As sf author and historian Brian Stableford points out in his 1989 essay "The Plausibility of the Impossible," the universe we discovered by means of the scientific method in the early twentieth century defies common sense: "We are haunted by a sense of the impossibility of ultimately making sense of things." By playing host to certain far-out notions—time travel, faster-than-light travel, and ESP, for example—that we have every reason to judge impossible, science fiction serves as an "instrument of negotiation," Stableford suggests, with which we strive to accomplish "the difficult diplomacy of existence in a scientifically knowable but essentially unimaginable world." This is no less true today than during the Radium Age.

The social, cultural, political, and technological upheavals of the 1900–1935 period are reflected in the proto-sf writings of authors such as Olaf Stapledon, William Hope Hodgson, Muriel Jaeger, Karel Čapek, G. K. Chesterton, Cicely Hamilton, W. E. B. Du Bois, Yevgeny Zamyatin, E. V. Odle, Arthur Conan Doyle, Mikhail

Bulgakov, Pauline Hopkins, Stanisław Ignacy Witkiewicz, Aldous Huxley, Gustave Le Rouge, A. Merritt, Rudyard Kipling, Rose Macaulay, J. D. Beresford, J. J. Connington, S. Fowler Wright, Jack London, Thea von Harbou, and Edgar Rice Burroughs, not to mention the late-period but still incredibly prolific H. G. Wells himself. More cynical than its Victorian precursor yet less hard-boiled than the sf that followed, in the writings of these visionaries we find acerbic social commentary, shock tactics, and also a sense of frustrated idealism—and reactionary cynicism, too—regarding humankind's trajectory.

The MIT Press's Radium Age series represents a much-needed evolution of my own efforts to champion the best proto-sf novels and stories from 1900 to 1935 among scholars already engaged in the fields of utopian and speculative fiction studies, as well as general readers interested in science, technology, history, and thrills and chills. By reissuing literary productions from a time period that hasn't received sufficient attention for its contribution to the emergence of science fiction as a recognizable form—one that exists and has meaning in relation to its own traditions and innovations, as well as within a broader ecosystem of literary genres, each of which, as John Rieder notes in *Science Fiction and the Mass Cultural Genre System* (2017), is itself a product of overlapping "communities of practice"—we hope not only to draw attention to key overlooked works but perhaps also to influence the way scholars and sf fans alike think about this crucial yet neglected and misunderstood moment in the emergence of the sf genre.

John W. Campbell and other Cold War–era sf editors and propagandists dubbed a select group of writers and story types from the pulp era to be the golden age of science fiction. In doing so, they helped fix in the popular imagination a too-narrow understanding of what the sf genre can offer. (In his introduction to the 1974 collection *Before the Golden Age*, for example, Isaac Asimov notes that although it may have possessed a certain exuberance, in general sf from before the mid-1930s moment when Campbell assumed editorship of *Astounding Stories* "seems, to anyone who has experienced the Campbell Revolution, to be clumsy, primitive, naive.") By returning to an international tradition of scientific speculation via fiction from after the Poe–Verne–Wells era and before sf's Golden Age, the Radium Age series will demonstrate—contra Asimov et al.—the breadth, richness, and diversity of the literary works that were responding to a vertiginous historical period, and how they helped innovate a nascent genre (which wouldn't be named until the mid-1920s, by Hugo Gernsback, founder of *Amazing Stories* and namesake of the Hugo Awards) as a mode of speculative imagining.

The MIT Press's Noah J. Springer and I are grateful to the sf writers and scholars who have agreed to serve as this series' advisory board. Aided by their guidance, we'll endeavor to surface a rich variety of texts, along with introductions by a diverse group of sf scholars, sf writers, and others that will situate these remarkable, entertaining, forgotten works within their own social, political, and scientific contexts, while drawing out contemporary parallels.

We hope that reading Radium Age writings, published in times as volatile as our own, will serve to remind us that our own era's seemingly natural, eternal, and inevitable social, economic, and cultural forms and norms are—like Madame Curie's atom—forever in flux.

INTRODUCTION
"THE WARS OF THE AIR AND THE LABORATORY": *THEODORE SAVAGE* AT 100

Susan R. Grayzel

As an account of modern warfare, *Theodore Savage* is simultaneously prescient and rooted in its post–First World War moment. And as the story of the fate of its middle-class, English title character and his society, the book offers a feminist dystopia by demonstrating what totalizing war can do to women—by silencing the voices of anyone resembling its author, Cicely Hamilton, or her similarly educated, motivated circle of women writers, artists, and activists.

Cicely Hamilton is perhaps best known for her 1909 treatise *Marriage as a Trade*, a scathing analysis of the marital relationship for women. Born in London in 1872, she came of age at a moment when middle-class women had gained greater access to education and yet remained highly limited in their economic prospects, as she would discover in her own life. Forced to support herself from the age of 19, Hamilton left teaching to pursue a career on the stage, then turned to writing plays. In this pursuit, she found enough success that she would become a valuable asset to the intensifying prewar women's suffrage campaign—in particular as a core member of the Women's Freedom League, an organization devoted as much to social justice and alleviating the condition of ordinary women as it was to securing the right to vote.

Hamilton's writing would always possess a feminist slant, defending the rights of women to independence and a public voice. After the First World War, however, the content and focus of her writing shifted decisively. Her wartime publications—*Senlis* (1917), a work of nonfiction recounting the devastation of France and the abuses of French civilians by the German army, and the novel *William—An Englishman* (1919), the story of a young, politically engaged English couple who, while honeymooning in Belgium in 1914, encounter the brutality of the enemy—both decry the failure of the invading military to live up to "rules of war." Yet Hamilton's critique of war's horrors is not necessarily unique to the First World War's new circumstances. The decision to expose the damage caused by that war's innovations evolved out of her own firsthand experiences in the war's final year.

While working in Abbeville during Germany's spring offensive of 1918, Hamilton bore witness to modern warfare's new and improved capacity to devastate civilian spaces and lives. As she recounts in her 1935 autobiography, *Life Errant*, she had an epiphany during one "red wicked night" sheltering in the countryside after fleeing Abbeville:

> In the old wars men sheltered behind walls and found safety in numbers. . . . But in our wars, the wars of the air and the laboratory, the wall, like enough, is a trap that you fly from to the open, and there is danger, not safety, in numbers— the crowd is a target to the terror that strikes from above. All the country, nightly, was alive with men and women who, in obedience to the principles of the new warfare, had fled from

the neighborhood of the target—the town—and scattered in small groups that they might be ignored and invisible. . . . [W]hat we saw was but a promise of terror to come.

In the years following the war, the damage wrought by modern, scientific warfare preoccupied Hamilton. *Theodore Savage* (1922), published when she was 50, and *Lest Ye Die* (1928), a revised and expanded version written for an American publisher, embody her critique.

Hamilton's eerie capturing of the destructive potential and terror of the aerial wars that followed 1918 is notable, given the ways in which images of civilians taking shelter from bombing raids have dominated our sense of wars ever since up until the present day images from Ukraine. Like other interwar texts, *Theodore Savage* imagines the tactics of such wars carried to their logical end—the destruction of town, city, civil society, and modern life. The fate of women in such a world preoccupied her.

In *Marriage as a Trade*, Hamilton lays bare the many ways in which marriage is primarily an economic arrangement. For Hamilton, marriage for women represents "the exchange of her person for the means of subsistence," and tragically never occurs for her "profit" or benefit. This exchange has severely limited the opportunities for women to be fully alive, independent, and, most importantly, free, and part of the joy of Hamilton's snide commentary lies in its insistence that there is nothing inherent or natural in women taking up marriage as an occupation—they must be trained for it like any other. Tearing apart any argument presented as to why women should choose to participate in this trade, she instead calls for a world where a woman can stand for herself, "fighting her own battle[s]" in any sphere of life while acknowledging that the failure to have reached such a world is due in part to women's own complicity. Hamilton's prewar lament that so few women can imagine a future where they are truly free is crucial for understanding the domestic aspects of the drama that plays out in *Theodore Savage*.

*

Hamilton's titular protagonist is a specific type of Englishman, an Oxford graduate working as a senior clerk in the civil service; someone so average that the book's first line informs us that "he would have been the first to admit that the interest of the record [of his life] lay in circumstance and not in himself." The portrayal of Theodore's prime of life, of the minutiae of clerkship seems evocative of Hamilton's own early wartime experiences, which she spent ably doing administrative work for the suffragist-inspired Scottish Women's Hospital in France. Theodore's existence is little more than a series of forms to be filled, rules to be followed, and order to be maintained so that society might continue functioning.

Theodore and his fellow civil servants pay scant attention to the far-off international tensions that lead to a declaration of war. Since he works for the "distribution office," he is sent north, to York, to ensure that food and supplies reach both the military units and the civilian population. On the eve of his departure, he gets an inkling of the technological terrors that this war might entail when he meets up with Markham, a chemist, who explains that "You can't combine the practice of science and the art of war; in the end, it's one or the other."

With these prophetic words, the story shifts from the anticipated war to the war's official outbreak—which at first feels like something far away, almost inconsequential. That changes "the night when disaster began," with fires and flashes that turn the sky red—and quickly following this, with the huge displacement of the human population, "the second red night . . . the refugees appeared in their thousands—a horde of human rats driven out of their holes by terror, by fire and by gas." Poisonous fire sweeps through fields, destroying the foodstuffs in its path. The city of York is overwhelmed not by foreign invaders but by these refugees. The distribution office soon has no food or other supplies to distribute, and within days "order," the cornerstone of Theodore's world, has "ceased to exist."

Reassigned to a local garrison, Theodore observes how quickly society crumbles—"laws, systems, habits of body and mind . . . gone, leaving nothing but animal fear and the animal need to be fed." As society's laws, systems, and habits crumble, Hamilton helps us understand the fragile state of equality between the sexes, and of the rights of women in general:

> Once a score or so of women, with a tall, frantic girl as their leader, stood for hours at the edge of the wire entanglement and called on the soldiers to shoot—if they would not feed them, to shoot. . . . More dreadful . . . were those who sought to bribe the possessors of food with the remnant of

their feminine attractions . . . The price for those who traded their bodies was paid in a hunk of bread or meat. . . . Those women suffered most who had no man of their own to forage or fend for them, and were no longer young enough for other men to look on them with pleasure.

All too soon, the position of women in wartime England descends to a place where subsistence is the best they can hope for—and only those with bodies worth desiring can trade for that. Modern warfare has laid bare the fragility of women's ability to do anything independently.

Reduced to burrowing for shelter and scrounging for food, Theodore joins the starving rabble. One night, fleeing from a temporary community that has been attacked, he finds himself on the run with a young woman, Ada, for whom he reluctantly takes responsibility. Everything we learn about Ada comes from Theodore's perspective—she is above all dependent, unable to be alone or to think for herself.

A few details emerge as the duo wanders in search of food and shelter across a ravaged landscape. She's an ex-factory hand with a Cockney accent. "Vulgarly harmless," she only comes alive when Theodore scavenges some remnants of lace and embroidery for her. Ada is an avatar of women trained, by society, for marriage as a trade. The aim of Ada's prewar life, Hamilton would have us understand, was merely to make herself attractive enough to gain a husband and leave the factory. She would happily have given up what independence her wages might have brought in exchange for the subsistence of plying her "natural" trade.

Alone together, Theodore and Ada "settle down swiftly and prosaically into a married state," one with a rigid division of labor. The adjective most often applied to Ada is "helpless," along with "superficial" and "unresourceful." Theodore learns to forage, becoming a hunter and a gatherer, but Ada can't even boil water. Exasperated at her failure to follow his simple instructions, Theodore finally beats Ada—who is thus "trained" to obey him, even as Theodore accepts his role as her "master."

*

The events of the last third of the novel, which take place two years later, are driven by Ada's pregnancy. Seeking out a community that includes women who can help Ada deliver the baby, Theodore discovers an established group that requires him to forswear "devil's knowledge"—that is to say, any understanding of science or engineering. For "what these outcasts, these remnants of humanity feared above all things was a revival of science, the mechanical powers that had wrecked their cities, their houses, and their lives." Ada and Theodore's children, Hamilton intones, all "inherit ignorance as a birthright."

An indifferent mother and worker, Ada is good at little in the community. She is a worse wife—although when Theodore witnesses her being accused of infidelity, his response is inspired more by an "outraged sense of property" and disinclination to support another man's child than it is by jealousy. When Ada dies, Theodore wastes little time in marrying "a sturdy young woman who had been broken to the duties required of her." Such a rigid enforcement of imbalanced gender relations, with women existing solely as domestic laborers, wives, and mothers, reflects Hamilton's worst fears.

Hamilton was one of a number of feminists who, in the aftermath of the First World War's use of air power and chemical weapons, warned not only of the horrors to be inflicted on soldiers but also of their consequences for humanity itself. As she would note in her autobiography, "when you have once accepted the more than possibility that your civilization is headed for destruction, it is almost inevitable that you will slip into indifference towards many ideas and interests and activities that would otherwise have seemed to you important." The idea of loss, of absolute "disaster through science" haunted her, she explains—and she saw it leading to a "barbaric" new way of life.

In some other proto-sf texts published before World War II, women are depicted as playing a more heroic role. The female characters in Maboth Moseley's *The War Upon Women* (1934) assassinate the man responsible for starting a highly modern war; the title character in George Cornwallis-West's *The Woman Who Stopped War* (1935) orchestrates a worldwide strike of women as war looms; and Lady Lysistrata, the protagonist of Eric Linklater's *The Impregnable Women* (1938), is a reference to Aristophanes' play about the women of warring cities who force their menfolk to negotiate peace by withholding sexual privileges, a story the novel updates.

Hamilton's vision, by contrast, offers little to suggest that women could do anything except try to survive.

Susan R. Grayzel

Among the catastrophes that emerge from her vision of modern war is the destruction of the feminist life that Hamilton herself experienced—in her words an "errant" life. Hamilton was able to live independently until her death, earning her keep with her pen and voice and contributing to society. She does not place herself, or any version of herself, in *Theodore Savage*—this is not the story of what happens to women like her. But by vocalizing a critique of the dangers that science and human hubris coupled with violence could unleash on the world, by showing us the immense fragility of gender equality alongside the fragility of the modern state and of life itself, at 100 years of age, Hamilton's novel may still have something to teach us.

I

If it had been possible for Theodore Savage to place on record for those who came after him the story of his life and experiences, he would have been the first to admit that the interest of the record lay in circumstance and not in himself. From beginning to end he was much what surroundings made of him; in his youth the product of a public school, Wadham and the Civil Service; in maturity and age a toiler with his hands in the company of men who lived brutishly. In his twenties, no doubt, he was frequently bored by his clerking duties and the routine of the Distribution Office; later on there were seasons when all that was best in him cried out against confinement in a life that had no aspiration; but neither boredom nor resentment ever drove him to revolt or set him to the moulding of circumstance. If he was destined to live as a local tradition and superman of legend, the honour was not gained by his talents or personal achievements; he had to thank for it an excellent constitution, bequeathed him by his parents, certain traces of refinement in manner and speech and the fears of very ignorant men.

When the Distribution Office—like his Hepplewhite furniture, his colour-prints and his English glass—was with yesterday's seven thousand years, it is more than possible that Theodore Savage, looking back on his youth, saw existence, till he neared the age of thirty, as a stream of scarcely ruffled content. Sitting crouched to the fire in the sweat-laden air of his cabin or humped idly on a hillside in the dusk of summer evening, it may well have seemed, when his thoughts strayed backwards, that the young man who once was impossibly himself was a being whom care did not touch. What he saw with the eye of his mind and memory was a neat young Mr. Savage who was valeted in comfortable chambers and who worked, without urgence, for limited hours, in a room that looked on Whitehall. Who in his plentiful leisure gained a minor reputation on the golf-links! Who frequented studios, bought—now and then—a picture and collected English glass and bits of furniture. Who was passably good-looking, in an ordinary way, had a thoughtful taste in socks and ties and was careful of his hands as a woman. . . . So—through the vista of years and the veil of contrast—Theodore may have seen his young manhood; and in time, perhaps, it was difficult for a coarse-fingered labourer, dependent for his bread on the moods of nature, to sympathize greatly with the troubles of neat Mr. Savage or think of him as subject to the major afflictions of humanity.

All the same, he would spend long hours in communion with his vanished self; striving at times to trace resemblances between the bearded, roughened features that a fishing-pool reflected and the smooth-chinned civil servant with brushed hair and white collar whom he followed in thought through his work, his amusements, his love-making and the trivial details of existence. . . .

And imagining, sometimes, the years and the happenings that might have been if his age, like his youth, had been soaped and collared, routined by his breeding and his office; if gods and men had not run amuck in frenzy and his sons had been born of a woman who lived delicately—playing Chopin of an evening to young Mr. Savage and giving him cream in his tea? . . .

Even if life in his Civil Service days was not all that it shone through the years of contrast, Theodore Savage could have had very little of hardship to complain of in the days when he added to a certain amount of private income a salary earned by the duties of the unexacting billet which a family interest had secured for him. If he had no particular vocation for the bureaucratic life—if good painting delighted, and official documents bored him—he had sufficient common sense to understand that it is given to most of us, with sufficient application, to master the intricacies of official documents, while only to few is it given to master an art. After a phase of abortive experiment in his college days he had realized—fortunately—that his swift and instinctive pleasure in beauty had in it no creative element; whereupon he settled down, early and easily, into the life and habits of the amateur. . . . There remained with him to the end of his days an impression of a young man living pleasurably, somewhat fastidiously; pursuing his hobbies, indulging his tastes, on the whole without much damage to himself or to others affected; acting decently according to his code and, when he fell in love and out of it, falling not too grossly or disastrously. If he had a grievance against his work at the Distribution Office, it was no more serious than this: it took much time, certain hours every day, from the interests that counted in his life. And against that grievance, no doubt, he set the ameliorating fact that his private means unaided would hardly have supported his way of existence, his many pleasant interests and himself; it was his civil servant's salary that had furnished his rooms in accordance with his taste and made possible the purchase of his treasured Fragonard and his bell-toned Georgian wine-glasses. . . . The bearded toiler, through a mist of years, watched a young man dawdling, without fear of the future, through a world of daily comforts that to his sons would seem fantastic, the creation of legend or of dream.

It was that blind and happy lack of all fear of the future that lent interest to the toiler's watching; knowing what he knew of the years that lay ahead, there was something of grim and dramatic humour in the sight of himself—yea, Theodore Savage, the broken-nailed, unshorn—arrayed of a morning in a flowered silk dressing-gown or shirt-fronted for an evening at the opera. . . . As it was in the beginning, is now and ever shall be—that, so it seemed to him in later years, had been the real, if unspoken, motto of the world wherein he had his being in the days of his unruffled content. . . .

Of the last few weeks in the world that was and ever should be he recalled, on the whole, very little of great hurrying and public events; it was the personal, intimate scenes that stood out and remained to a line and a detail. His first meeting with Phillida Rathbone, for instance, and the chance interview with her father that led to it: he could see himself standing by Rathbone's desk in the Distribution Office, see the bowl between his fingers, held to the light—see its very shape and conventional pattern of raised flowers.

Rathbone—John Rathbone—was his chief in his Distribution days; a square-jawed, formidable, permanent official who was held in awe by underlings and Ministers, and himself was subject, most contentedly subject, to a daughter, the ruler of his household. Her taste in art and decoration was not her father's, but, for all the bewilderment it caused him, he strove to gratify it loyally; and for Phillida's twenty-third birthday he had chosen expensively, on his way to the office, at the shop of a dealer in antiquities. Swept on the spate of the dealer's eloquence he had been pleased for the moment with his find—a flowered bowl, reputed Chelsea; it was not until half an hour later that he remembered uneasily his daughter's firm warnings against unaided traffic with the miscreants who deal in curios. With the memory uncomfortable doubts assailed him, while previous experiments came thronging unpleasantly to mind—the fiasco of the so-called Bartolozzi print and the equally lamentable business of the so-called Chippendale settee. . . . He drew his purchase from its paper wrapping, set it down on the table and stared at it. The process brought no enlightenment and he was still wrestling with uncomfortable doubts when Theodore Savage knocked and came in with a draft report for approval.

The worry born of ignorance faded out of Rathbone's face as he conned the document and amended its clauses with swift pencilled notes in the margin; he was back with the solidities he knew and could make sense of, and superfluous gimcracks for the moment had ceased to exist. It was Savage who unwittingly recalled their existence and importance; when his chief, at the end of his corrections, looked up, the younger man was eyeing the troublesome gimcrack with a meditative interest that reminded Rathbone of his daughter's manner when she contemplated similar rubbish.

"Know anything about old china?" he inquired—an outward and somewhat excessive indifference concealing an inward anxiety.

"Not much," said Theodore modestly; but, taking the query as request for an opinion, his hand went out to the bowl.

"What do you make of it?" asked Rathbone, still blatantly indifferent. "I picked it up this morning—for my daughter. Supposed to be Chelsea—should you say it was?"

If the answer had been in the negative the private acquaintance between chief and subordinate would probably have made no further progress; no man, even when he makes use of it, is grateful for the superior knowledge in a junior that convicts him to his face of gullibility. As it was, the verdict was favourable and Rathbone, in the relief of finding that he had not blundered, grew suddenly friendly—to the point of a dinner invitation; which was given, in part, as instinctive thanks for restored self-esteem, in part because it might interest Phillida to meet a young man who took gimcracks as gravely as herself. The invitation, as a matter of course, was accepted; and three days later Savage met Phillida Rathbone.

"I've asked a young fellow you're sure to get on with"—so Rathbone had informed his daughter; who, thereupon, as later she confessed to Theodore, had made up her mind to be bored. She threw away her prejudice swiftly when she found the new acquaintance talked music with intelligence—she herself had music in her brain as well as in her finger-tips—while he from the beginning was attracted by a daintiness of manner and movement that puzzled him in Rathbone's daughter. . . . From that first night he must have been drawn to her, since the evening remained to him clear in every detail; always in the hollow of a glowing fire he could summon up Phillida, himself and Rathbone, sitting, the three of them, round the table with its silver and tall roses. . . . In the centre a branching cluster of roses—all yellow, like Phillida's dress. . . . Rathbone, for the most part, good-naturedly silent, Phillida and himself talking swiftly. . . . In shaded light and a solid, pleasant comfort; ordinary comfort, which he took for granted as an element of daily life, but which yet was the heritage of many generations, the product of long centuries of striving and cunning invention. . . . Later, in the drawing-room, the girl made music—and he saw himself listening from his corner of the sofa with a cigarette, unlit, between his fingers. Above all it was her quality of daintiness that pleased him; she was a porcelain girl, with something of the grace that he associated with the eighteenth century. . . .

After half an hour that was sheer content to Theodore she broke off from her playing to sit on the arm of her father's chair and ruffle his grey hair caressingly.

"Old man, does my noise on the piano prevent you from reading your paper?"

Whereat Rathbone laughed and returned the caress; and Phillida explained, for the visitor's benefit, that the poor dear didn't know one tune from another and must have been bored beyond measure—by piano noises since they came upstairs and nothing but music-talk at dinner.

"I believe we've driven him to the Montagu divorce case," she announced, looking over his shoulder. "'Housemaid cross-examined—the Colonel's visits.' Daddy, have you fallen to that?"

"No, minx," he rebuked her, "I haven't. I'm not troubling to wade through the housemaid's evidence for the very good reason that it's quite unnecessary. I shall hear all about it from you."

"That's a nasty one," Phillida commented, rubbing her cheek against her father's. She turned the paper idly, reading out the headlines. "'American elections—Surprises at Newmarket—Bank Rate'—There doesn't seem much news except the housemaid and the colonel, does there?"

Rathbone laughed as he pinched her cheek and pointed—to a headline here and a headline there, to a cloud that was not yet the size of a man's hand.

"It depends on what you call news. It seems to have escaped you that we've just had a Budget. That matters to those of us who keep expensive daughters. And, little as the subject may interest you, I gather from the size of his type, that the editor attaches some importance to the fact that the Court of Arbitration has decided against the Karthanian claim. That, of course, compared to a housemaid in the witness-box is——"

"Ponderous," she finished and laughed across at Theodore. "Important, no doubt, but ponderous—the Court of Arbitration always is. That's why I skipped it." . . . Then, carelessly interested, and running her eye down the columns of the newspaper, she supposed the decision was final and those noisy little Karthanians would have to be quiet at last. Rathbone shrugged his shoulders and hoped so.

"But they'll have to, won't they?" said Phillida. "Give me a match, Daddy—There's no higher authority than the Court of Arbitration, is there?"

"If," Rathbone suggested as he held a light to her cigarette, "if your newspaper reading were not limited to scandals and chiffons, you might have noticed that your noisy little friends in the East have declared with their customary vehemence that in no circumstances whatever will they accept an adverse verdict—not even from the Court of Arbitration."

"But they'll have to, won't they?" Phillida repeated placidly. "I mean—they can't go against everybody else. Against the League."

She tried to blow a smoke-ring with conspicuous ill-success, and Theodore, watching her from his corner of the sofa—intent on her profile against the light—heard Rathbone explaining that "against everybody else" was hardly the way to put it, since the Federal Council was not a happy family at present. There was very little doubt that Karthania was being encouraged to make trouble—and none at all that there would be difference of opinion on the subject of punitive action. . . . Phillida, with an arm round her father's neck, was divided between international politics and an endeavour to make the perfect ring—now throwing in a question anent the constitution and dissensions of the League, now rounding her mouth for a failure—while Theodore, on the sofa, leaned his head upon his hand that he might shade his eyes and watch her without seeming to watch. . . . He listened to Rathbone—and did not listen; and that, as he realized later, had been so far his attitude to interests in the mass. The realities of his life were immediate and personal—with, in the background, dim interests in the mass that were vaguely distasteful as politics. A collective game played with noisy idealism and flaring abuse, which served as copy to the makers of newspapers and gave rise at intervals to excited conversation and argument. . . .

What was real, and only real while Rathbone talked, was the delicate poise of Phillida's head, the decorative line of Phillida's body, his pleasure in the sight of her, his comfort in a well-ordered room; these things were realities, tangible or æsthetic, in whose company a man, if he were so inclined, might discuss academically an Eastern imbroglio and the growing tendency to revolt against the centralized authority of the League. Between life, as he grasped it, and public affairs there was no visible, essential connection. The Karthanian imbroglio, as he strolled to his chambers, was an item in the make-up of a newspaper, the subject of a recent conversation; it was the rhythm of Phillida's music that danced in his brain as a living and insistent reality. That, and not the stirrings of uneasy nations, kept him wakeful till long after midnight.

II

While Theodore Savage paid his court to Phillida Rathbone, the Karthanian decision was the subject of more than conversation; diplomatists and statesmen were busy while he drifted into love and dreamed through the sudden rumours that excited his fellows at the office. In London, for the most part, journalism was guarded and reticent, the threat of secession at first hardly mentioned; but in nations and languages that favoured secession the press was voicing the popular cry with enthusiasm that grew daily more heated. Through conflicting rumour this at least was clear: at the next meeting of the Council of the League its authority would be tested to the uttermost, since the measure of independent action demanded by the malcontent members would amount to a denial of the federal principle, to secession in fact if not in name. . . . Reaction against central and unified authority was not a phenomenon of yesterday; it had been gathering its strength through years of racial friction, finding an adherent in every community that considered itself aggrieved by a decision of the Council or award of the Court of Arbitration, and for years it had taxed the ingenuity of the majority of the Council to avoid open breach and defiance.

Before open breach and its consequences, both sides had so far manœuvred, hesitated, compromised; it had been left to a minor, a very minor, state, to rush in where others feared to tread. The flat refusal of a heady, half-civilized little democracy to accept the unfavourable verdict of the Court of Arbitration was the spark that might fire a powder-barrel; its frothy demonstrations, ridiculous in themselves, appealed to the combative instinct in others, to race-hatreds, old herding feuds and jealousies. These found vent in answering demonstrations, outbursts of popular sympathy in states not immediately affected; the noisy rebel was hailed as a martyr and pioneer of freedom, and became the pretext for resistance to the Council's oppression. There was no doubt of the extent of the re-grouping movement of the nations, of the stirrings of a widespread combativeness which denounced Federation as a system whereby dominant interests and races exploited their weaker rivals. With the meeting of the Council would come the inevitable clash of interests; the summons to the offending member of the League to retreat from its impossible position, and—in case of continued defiance—the proposal to take punitive action. That proposal, to all seeming, must bring about a crisis; those members of the League who had encouraged the rebel in defiance would hardly consent to co-operate in punitive measures; and refusal—withdrawal of their military contingents—would mean virtual secession and denial of majority rule. If collective excitement and anger ran high, it might mean even more than secession; there were possibilities—first hinted at, later discussed without subterfuge—of actual and armed opposition should the Council attempt to enforce its decree and authority. . . . Humanity, once more, was gathering into herds and growing sharply conscious alike of division and comradeship.

It was some time before Theodore was even touched by the herding instinct and spirit; apart, in a delicate world of his own, he concerned himself even less than usual with the wider interests of politics. By his fellows in the Distribution Office he was known as an incurable optimist; even when the cloud had spread rapidly and darkened he saw "strained relations" through the eyes of a lover, and his mind, busied elsewhere, refused to dwell anxiously on "incidents" and "disquieting possibilities." They intruded clumsily on his delicate world and, so soon as might be, he thrust them behind him and slipped back to the seclusion that belonged to himself and a woman. All his life, thought and impulse, for the time being, was a negation, a refusal of the idea of strife and destruction; in his happy egoism he planned to make and build—a home and a lifetime of content.

Now and again, and in spite of his reluctance, his veil of happy egoism was brushed aside—some chance word or incident forcing him to look upon the menace. There was the evening in Vallance's rooms, for instance—where the talk settled down to the political crisis, and Holt, the long journalist, turned sharply on Vallance, who supposed we were drifting into war.

"That's nonsense, Vallance! Nonsense! It's impossible—unthinkable!"

"Unpleasant, if you like," said Vallance; "but not impossible. At least—it never has been."

"That's no reason," Holt retorted; "we're not living yesterday. There'll be no war, and I'll tell you why: because the men who will have to start it—daren't!" He had a penetrating voice which he raised when excited, so that other talk died down and the room was filled with his argument. Politicians, he insisted, might bluff and use threats—menace with a bogy, shake a weapon they dared not use—but they would stop short at threats, manœuvre for position and retreat. Let loose modern science, mechanics and chemistry, they could not—there was a limit to human insanity, if only because there was a limit to the endurance of the soldier. Unless you supposed that all politicians were congenital idiots or criminal lunatics out to make holocausts. What was happening at present was manœuvring pure and simple; neither side caring to prejudice its case by open admission that appeal to force was unthinkable, each side hoping that the other would be the first to make the admission, each side trotting out the dummy soldiers that were only for show, and would soon be put back in their boxes. . . . War, he repeated, was unthinkable. . . .

"Man," said a voice behind Theodore, "does much that is unthinkable!"

Theodore turned that he might look at the speaker—Markham, something in the scientific line, who had sat in silence, with a pipe between his lips, till he dropped out his slow remark.

"Your mistake," he went on, "lies in taking these people—statesmen, politicians—for free agents, and in thinking they have only one fear. Look at Meyer's speech this morning—that's significant. He has been moderate so far, a restraining influence; now he breathes fire and throws in his lot with the extremists. What do you make of that?"

"Merely," said Holt, "that Meyer has lost his head."

"In which happy state," suggested Vallance, "the impossible and unthinkable mayn't frighten him."

"That's one explanation," said Markham. "The other is that he is divided between his two fears—the fear of war and the fear of his democracy, which, being in a quarrelsome and restless mood, would break him if he flinched and applauds him to the echo when he blusters. And, maybe, at the moment, his fear of being broken is greater than his fear of the impossible—at any rate the threat is closer. . . . The man himself may be reasonable—even now—but he is the instrument of instinctive emotion. Almost any man, taken by himself, is reasonable—and, being reasonable, cautious. Meyer can think, just as well as you and I, so long as he stands outside a crowd; but neither you nor I, nor Meyer, can think when we are one with thousands and our minds are absorbed into a jelly of impulse and emotion."

"I like your phrase about jelly," said Vallance. "It has an odd picturesqueness. Your argument itself—or, rather, your assertion—strikes me as a bit sweeping."

"All the same," Markham nodded, "it's worth thinking over. . . . Man in the mass, as a crowd, can only feel; there is no such thing as a mass-mind or intellect—only mass desires and emotions. That is what I mean by saying that Meyer—whatever his intelligence or sanity—is the instrument of instinctive emotion. . . . And instinctive emotion,

Holt—until it has been hurt—is damnably and owlishly courageous. It isn't clever enough to be afraid; not even of red murder—or starvation by the million—or the latest thing in gas or high explosive. Stir it up enough and it'll run on 'em—as the lemmings run to the sea."

Holt snorted something that sounded like "Rot!" and Vallance, sprawling an arm along the mantelpiece, asked, "Another of your numerous theories?"

"If you like," Markham assented, "but it's a theory deduced from hard facts. . . . It's a fact, isn't it, that no politician takes a crowd into his confidence until he wants to make a fight of it? It's a fact, isn't it, that no movements in mass are creative or constructive—that simultaneous action, simultaneous thought, always is and must be destructive? Set what we call the People in motion and something has got to be broken. The crowd-life is still at the elementary, the animal stage; it has not yet acquired the human power of construction . . . and the crowd, the people, democracy—whatever you like to call it—has been stirring in the last few years; getting conscious again, getting active, looking round for something to break . . . which means that the politician is faced once more with the necessity of giving it something to break. Naturally he prefers that the breakage should take place in the distance—and, League or no League, the eternal and obvious resource is War . . . which was not too risky when fought with swords and muskets, but now—as Holt says—is impossible. Being a bit of a chemist, I'm sure Holt is right; but I'm also sure that man, as a herd, does not think. Further, I am doubtful if man, as a herd, ever finds out what is impossible except through the painful process of breaking his head against it."

"I'm a child in politics," said Vallance, "and I may be dense—but I'm afraid it isn't entirely clear to me whether your views are advanced or grossly and shamelessly reactionary?"

"Neither," said Markham, "or both—you can take your choice. I have every sympathy with the people, the multitude; it's hard lines that it can only achieve destruction—just because there is so much of it, because it isn't smaller. But I also sympathize with the politician in his efforts to control the destructive impulse of the multitude. And, finally—in view of that progress of science of which Holt has reminded us, and of which I know a little myself—I'm exceedingly sorry for us all."

Someone from across the room asked: "You make it war, then?"

"I make it war. We have had peace for more than a generation, so our periodic blood-letting is already a long time overdue. The League has staved it off for a bit, but it hasn't changed the human constitution; and the real factor in the Karthanian quarrel—or any other—is the periodic need of the human herd for something to break and for something to break itself against. . . . Resistance and self-sacrifice—the need of them—the call of the lemming to the sea. . . . And, perhaps, it's all the stronger in this generation because this generation has never known war, and does not fear it."

"Education," said Holt, addressing the air, "is general and compulsory—has been so for a good many years. The inference being that the records of previous wars—and incidentally of the devastation involved—are not inaccessible to that large proportion of our population which is known as the average man."

"As printed pages, yes," Markham agreed. "But what proportion even of a literate population is able to accept the statement of a printed page as if it were a personal experience?"

"As we're not all fools," Holt retorted, "I don't make it war."

"I hope you're right, for my own sake," said Markham good-temperedly. He knocked out his pipe as he spoke and made ready to go—while Theodore looked after him, interested, for the moment, disturbingly. . . . Markham's unemotional and matter-of-fact acceptance of "periodic blood-letting" made rumour suddenly real, and for the first time Theodore saw the Karthanian imbroglio as more than the substance of telegrams and articles, something human, actual, and alive. . . . Saw himself, even Phillida, concerned in it—through a medley of confused and threatening shadows. . . . For the moment he was roused from his self-absorption and thrust into the world that he shared with the common herd of men. He and Phillida were no longer as the gods apart, with their lives to make in Eden; they were little human beings, the sport of a common human destiny. . . . He remembered how eagerly he caught at Holt's condemnation of Markham as a crank and Vallance's next comment on the crisis.

"We had exactly the same scare three—or was it four?— years ago. This is the trouble about Transylvania all over again—just the same alarums and excursions. That fizzled out quietly in a month or six weeks and the chances are that Karthania will fizzle out, too."

"Of course it will," Holt declared with emphasis—and proceeded to demolish Markham's theories. Theodore left before he had finished his argument; as explained dogmatically in Holt's penetrating voice, the intrigues and dissensions of the Federal Council were once more unreal and frankly boring. The argument satisfied, but no longer interested—and ten minutes after Markham's departure his thoughts had drifted away from politics to the private world he shared with Phillida Rathbone.

For very delight of it he lingered over his courtship, finding charm in the pretence of uncertainty long after it had ceased to exist. To Phillida also there was pleasure not only in the winning, but in the exquisite game itself; once or twice when Theodore was hovering near avowal, she deferred the inevitable, eluded him with laughter, asked tacitly to play a little longer. . . . In the end the avowal came suddenly, on the flash and impulse of a moment— when Phillida hesitated over one of his gifts, a print she had admired on the wall of his sitting-room, duly brought the next day for her acceptance.

"No, I oughtn't to take it—it's one of your treasures," she remonstrated.

"If you'd take all I have—and me with it," he stammered. . . . That was the crisis of the exquisite game—and pretence of uncertainty was over.

III

One impression of those first golden hours that stayed with him always was the certainty with which they had dwelt on the details of their common future; he could see Phillida with her hands on his shoulders explaining earnestly that they must live very near to the Dad—the dear old boy had no one but herself and they mustn't let him miss her too much. And when Theodore asked, "You don't think he'll object to me?" Rathbone's disapproval was the only possible cloud—which lifted at Phillida's amused assurance that the old dear wasn't as blind as all that and, having objections, would have voiced them before it was too late.

"You don't suppose he hasn't noticed—just because he hasn't said anything!" . . . Whereupon Theodore caught at her hands and demanded how long she had noticed?—and they fell to a happy retracing of this step and that in their courtship.

When they heard Rathbone enter she ran down alone, telling Theodore to stay where he was till she called him; returning in five minutes or so, half-tearful and half-smiling, to say the dear old thing was waiting in the library. Then Theodore, in his turn, went down to the library where, red to the ears and stammering platitudes, he shook hands with his future father-in-law—proceeding eventually to details of his financial position and the hope that Rathbone would not insist upon too lengthy an engagement? . . . The answer was so slow in coming that he repeated his question nervously.

"No," said Rathbone at last, "I don't know that I"—(he laid stress on the pronoun)—"I don't know that I should insist upon a very lengthy engagement. Only. . . ."

Again he paused so long that Theodore repeated "Only?"

"Only—there may be obstacles—not of my making or Phillida's. Connected with the office—your work . . . I dare say you've been too busy with your own affairs to give very much attention to the affairs of the world in general; still I conclude the papers haven't allowed you to forget that the Federal Council was to vote to-day on the resolution to take punitive action? Result is just through—half an hour ago. Resolution carried, by a majority of one only."

"Was it?" said Theodore—and remembered a vague impulse of resentment, a difficulty in bringing down his thoughts from Phillida to the earthiness of politics. It took him an effort and a moment to add: "Close thing—but they've pulled it off."

"They have," said Rathbone. "Just pulled it off—but it remains to be seen if that's matter for congratulation. . . . The vote commits us to action—definitely—and the minority have entered a protest against punitive action. . . . It seems unlikely that the protest is only formal."

He was dry and curiously deliberate—leaning back in his chair, speaking quietly, with fingers pressed together

. . . . To the end Theodore remembered him like that; a square-jawed man, leaning back in his chair, speaking slowly, unemotionally—the harbinger of infinite misfortune. . . . And himself, the listener, a young man engrossed by his own new happiness; irritated, at first, by the intrusion of that which did not concern it; then (as once before in Vallance's rooms) uneasy and conscious of a threat.

He heard himself asking, "You think it's—serious?" and saw Rathbone's mouth twist into the odd semblance of a smile.

"I think so. One way or other we shall know within a week."

"You can't mean—war?" Theodore asked again— remembering Holt and his "Impossible!"

"It doesn't seem unlikely," said Rathbone.

He had risen, with his hands thrust deep into his pockets, and begun to pace backwards and forwards. "Something may happen at the last minute—but it's difficult to see how they can draw back. They have gone too far. They're committed, just as we are—committed to a principle. . . . If we yield the Council abdicates its authority once for all; it's an end of the League—a plain break, and the Lord knows what next. And the other side daren't stop at verbal protest. They will have to push their challenge; there's too much clamour behind them. . . ."

"There was Transylvania," Theodore reminded him.

"I know—and nothing came of it. But that wasn't pushed quite so far. . . . They threatened, but never definitely—they left themselves a possibility of retreat.

Now . . . as I said, something may happen . . . and, meanwhile, to go back to what I meant about you, personally, how this might affect you. . . ."

He dropped into swift explanation. "Considerable rearrangement in the work of the Department—if it should be necessary to place it on a war-footing." Theodore's duties—if the worst should happen—would certainly take him out of London and therefore part him from Phillida. "I can tell you that definitely—now."

Perhaps he realized that the announcement, on a day of betrothal, was brutal; for he checked himself suddenly in his walk to and fro, clapped the young man good-naturedly on the shoulder, repeated that "Something might happen" and supposed he would not be sorry to hear that a member of the Government required his presence—"So you and Phillida can dine without superfluous parents." . . . And he said no word of war or parting to Phillida—who came down with Theodore to watch her father off, standing arm-in-arm upon the doorstep in the pride of her new relationship.

The threat lightened as they dined alone deliciously, as a foretaste of housekeeping in common; Phillida left him no thoughts to stray and only once, while the evening lasted, did they look from their private Paradise upon the world of common humanity. Phillida, as the clock neared ten, wondered vaguely what Henderson had wanted with her father? Was there anything particular, did Theodore know, any news about the Federal Council? . . . He hesitated for a moment, then told her the bare facts only—the vote and the minority protest.

"A protest," she repeated. "That's what they've all been afraid of. . . . It looks bad, doesn't it?"

He agreed it looked bad; thinking less, it may be, of the threat of red ruin and disaster than of Rathbone's warning that his duties would part him from Phillida.

"I hope it doesn't mean war," she said.

At the time her voice struck him as serious, even anxious; later it amazed him that she had spoken so quietly, that there was no trembling of the slim white fingers that played with her chain of heavy beads.

"Do you think it does?" she asked him.

Because he remembered the threat of parting and had need of her daily presence, he was stubborn in declaring that it did not, and could not, mean war; quoting Holt that modern war was impossible, that statesmen and soldiers knew it, and insisting that this was the Transylvanian business over again and would be settled as that was settled. She shook her head thoughtfully, having heard other views from her father; but her voice (he knew later) was thoughtful only—not a quiver, not a hint of real fear in it.

"It'll have to come sometime—now or in a year or two. At least, that's what everybody says. I wonder if it's true."

"No," he said, "it isn't—unless we make it true. This sort of thing—it's a kind of common nightmare we have now and then. Every few years—and when it's over we turn round and wake up and wonder what the devil we were frightened about."

"Yes," she agreed, "when you come to think of it, it is rather like that. I don't remember in the least what the fuss was all about last time—but I know the papers were full of Transylvania and the poor old Dad was worked off his head for a week or two. . . . And then it was over and we forgot all about it."

And at that they turned and went back to their golden solitude, shutting out, for the rest of the evening, a world that made protests and sent ominous telegrams. Before Theodore left her, to walk home restless with delight, they had decided on the fashion of Phillida's ring and planned the acquisition of a Georgian house—with powder-closet.

It was his restless delight that made sleep impossible—and he sat at his window and smoked till the east was red. . . . While Henderson and Rathbone, a mile or two away, planned Distribution on a war-footing.

Events in the next few days moved rapidly in an atmosphere of tense and rising life; races and peoples were suddenly and acutely conscious of their life collective, and the neighbourly quarrel and bitterness of yesterday was forgotten in the new comradeship born of common hatred and common passion for self-sacrifice. There was talk at first, with diplomatists and leader-writers, of a possibility of localizing the conflict; but within forty-eight hours of the issue of the minority protest it was clear that the League would be rent. On one side, as on the other, statesmen were popular only when known to be unyielding in the face of impossible demands; crowds gathered when ministers met to take counsel and greeted them with cries to stand fast. Behind vulgar effervescence and music-hall thunder was faith in a righteous cause;

and, as ever, man believed in himself and his cause with a hand on the hilt of his sword. Freedom and justice were suddenly real and attainable swiftly—through violence wrought on their enemies. . . . Humanity, once more, was inspired by ideals that justified the shedding of blood and looked death in the face without fear.

As always, there were currents and crosscurrents, and those who were not seized by the common, splendid passion denounced it. Some meanly, by distortion of motive—crying down faith as cupidity and the impulse to self-sacrifice as arrogance; and others, more worthy of hearing, who realized that the impulse to self-sacrifice is passing and the idealism of to-day the bestial cunning of to-morrow. . . . On one side and the other there was an attempt on the part of those who foresaw something, at least, of the inevitable, to pit fear against the impulse to self-sacrifice and make clear to a people to whom war was a legend only the extent of disaster ahead. The attempt was defeated, almost as begun, by the sudden launching of an ultimatum with twenty-four hours for reply.

At the news young men surged to the recruiting-stations, awaiting their turn for admission in long shouting, jesting lines; the best blood and honour of a generation that had not yet sated its inborn lust of combat. Women stood to watch them as their ranks moved slowly to the goal—some proud to tears, others giggling a foolish approval. Great shifting crowds—men and women who could not rest—gathered in public places and awaited the inevitable news. In the last few hours—all protest being useless—even the loudest of the voices that clamoured against war had died down; and in the life collective was the strange, sudden peace which comes with the cessation of internal feud and the focusing of hatred on those who dwell beyond a nation's borders.

Theodore Savage, in the days that followed his betrothal, was kept with his nose to the Distributive grindstone, working long hours of overtime in an atmosphere transformed out of knowledge. The languid and formal routine of departments was succeeded by a fever of hurried innovation; gone were the lazy, semi-occupied hours when he had been wont to play with his thoughts of Phillida and the long free evenings that were hers as a matter of course. In the beginning he felt himself curiously removed from the strong, heady atmosphere that affected others like wine. Absorption in Phillida counted for something in his aloofness, but even without it his temperament was essentially averse from the crowd-life; he was stirred by the common desire to be of service, but was conscious of no mounting of energy restless and unsatisfied. . . . Having little conviction or bias in politics, he accepted without question the general version of the origins of conflict and resented, in orthodox fashion, the gross breach of faith and agreement which betrayed long established design. "It had got to be" and "They've been getting ready for years" were phrases on the general lip which he saw no reason to discredit; and, with acceptance of the inevitability of conflict, he ceased to find conflict "unthinkable." In daily intercourse with those to whom it was thinkable, practical, a certainty—to some, in the end, a desirable certainty—Holt's phrase lost its meaning and became a symbolic extravagance. . . . So far he was caught in the swirl of the crowd-life; but he was never one with it and remained conscious of it always as something that flowed by him, something apart from himself.

Above all he knew it as something apart when he saw how it had seized and mastered Phillida. She was curiously alive to its sweep and emotion, and beneath her outward daintiness lay the power of fervid partisanship. "If it weren't for you," she told him once, "I should break my heart because I'm only a woman"; and he saw that she pitied him, that she was even resentful for his sake, when she learned from her father that there was no question of allowing the clerks of the Distribution Office to volunteer for military service.

"He says the Department will need all its trained men and that modern war is won by organization even more than by fighting. I'm glad you won't have to go, my dear— I'm glad—" and, saying it, she clung to him as to one who stood in need of consolation.

He felt the implied consolation and sympathy—with a twinge of conscience, not entirely sure of deserving it. But for the rigid departmental order, he knew he should have thought it his duty to volunteer and take his share of the danger that others were clamouring to face; but he had not cursed vehemently, like his junior, Cassidy, when Holles, equally blasphemous, burst into the room with the news that enlistment was barred. He thought of Cassidy's angry blue eyes as he swore that, by hook or by crook, he would find his way into the air-service. . . . Phillida would have sympathized with Cassidy and the flash of her eyes answered his; she too, for the moment, was one with the crowd-life, and there were moments when he felt it was sweeping her away from his hold.

He felt it most on their last evening, on the night the ultimatum expired; when he came from the office, after hours of overtime, uncertain whether he should find her, wondering whether her excited restlessness had driven her out into the crowds that surged round Whitehall. As he ran up the stairs the sound of a piano drifted from the room above; no definite melody but a vague, irregular striking of chords that came to an end as he entered the room and Phillida looked up, expectant.

"At last," she said as she ran to him. "You don't know how I have wanted you. I can't be alone—if you hadn't turned up I should have had to find someone to talk to."

"Anyone—didn't matter who?" he suggested.

She laughed, caught his hand and rubbed her cheek against it. "Yes, anyone—you know what I mean. It's just—when you think of what's happening, how can you keep still? . . . As for father, I never see him nowadays. I suppose there isn't any news?"

"There can't be," he answered. "Not till twelve."

"No—and even at twelve it won't really be news. Just no answer—and the time will be up. . . . We're at peace now—till midnight. . . . What's the time?"

He longed to be alone with her—alone with her in thought as well as in outward seeming—but her talk slipped restlessly away from his leading and she moved uncertainly about the room, returning at last to her vague striking of the piano—sharp, isolated notes, and then suddenly a masterful chord.

"Play to me," he asked, "play properly."

She shook her head and declared it was impossible.

"Anything connected is beyond me; I can only strum and make noises." She crashed in the bass, rushed a swift arpeggio to the treble, then turned to him, her eyes wide and glowing. "If you hold your breath, can't you feel them all waiting?—thousands on thousands—all through the world? . . . Waiting till midnight . . . can't you feel it?"

"You make me feel it," he answered. "Tell me—you want war?"

The last words came out involuntarily, and it was only the startled, sudden change in her face that brought home to him what he had said.

"I want war," she echoed. . . . "I want men to be killed. . . . Theodore, what makes you say that?"

He fumbled for words, not sure of his own meaning—sure only that her eyes would change and lose their fervour if, at the last moment and by God-sent miracle, the sword were returned to its sheath.

"Not that, of course—not the actual fighting. I didn't mean that. . . . But isn't there something in you—in you and in everyone—that's too strong to be arrested? Too swift? . . . If nothing happened—if we drew back—you couldn't be still now; you couldn't endure it. . . ."

She looked at him thoughtfully, puzzled, half-assenting; then protested again: "I don't want it—but we can't be still and endure evil."

"No," he said, "we can't—but isn't there a gladness in the thought that we can't?"

"Because we're right," she flashed. "It's not selfish—you know it isn't selfish. We see what is right and, whatever it costs us, we stand for it. The greatest gladness of all is the gladness of giving—everything, even life. . . . That's what makes me wish I were a man!"

"The passion for self-sacrifice," he said, quoting Markham. "I was told the other day it was one of the causes of war. . . . Don't look at me so reproachfully—I'm not a pacifist. Give me a kiss and believe me."

She laughed and gave him the kiss he asked for, and for a minute or two he drew her out of the crowd-life and they were alone together as they had been on the night of their betrothal. Then the spirit of restlessness took hold of her again and she rose suddenly, declaring they must find out what was happening—they must go out and see for themselves.

"It's only just past ten," he argued. "What can be happening for another two hours? There'll only be a crowd—walking up and down and waiting."

It was just the crowd and its going to and fro that she needed, and she set to work to coax him out of his reluctance. There would never be another night like this one—they must see it together and remember it as long as they lived. . . . Perhaps, her point gained, she was remorseful, for she rewarded his assent with a caress and a coaxing apology.

"We shall have so many evenings to ourselves," she told him—"and to-night—to-night we don't only belong to ourselves."

He could feel her arm tremble and thrill on his own as they came in sight of the Clock Tower and the swarm of expectant humanity that moved and murmured round Westminster. On him the first impression was of seething insignificance that the Clock Tower dwarfed and the dignity of night reproved; on her, as he knew by the trembling of her fingers, a quickening of life and sensation. . . .

They were still at the shifting edges of the crowd when a man's voice called "Phillida!" and one of her undergraduate cousins linked himself on to their company. For nearly an hour the three moved backwards and forwards—through the hum and mutter of voices, the ceaseless turning of eyes to Big Ben and the shuffling of innumerable feet. . . . When the quarters chimed, there was always a hush; when eleven throbbed solemnly, no man stirred till the last beat died. . . . With silence and arrested movement the massed humanity at the base of the Clock Tower was no longer a seething insignificance; without speech, without motion, it was suddenly dignified—life faced with its destiny and intent upon a Moving Finger. . . .

"Only one more hour," whispered Phillida as the silence broke; and the Rathbone boy, to show he was not moved, wondered if it was worth their while to stay pottering about for an hour? . . . No one answered his question, since it needed no answer; and, the dignity of silence over, they drifted again with the crowd.

IV

The Moving Finger had written off another five minutes or so when police were suddenly active and sections of the crowd lunged uncomfortably; way was being made for the passing of an official car—and in the backward swirl of packed humanity Theodore was thrust one way, Phillida and the Rathbone boy another. For a moment he saw them as they looked round and beckoned him; the next, the swirl had carried him yet further—and when it receded they were lost amongst the drifting, shifting thousands. After ten minutes more of pushing to and fro in search of them, Theodore gave up the chase as fruitless and made his way disconsolately to the Westminster edge of the crowd. . . . Phillida, if he knew her, would stay till the stroke of midnight, later if the spirit moved her; and she had an escort in the Rathbone boy, who, in due time, would see her home. . . . There was no need to worry—but he cursed the luck of what might be their last evening.

For a time he lingered uncertainly on the edge of the pushing, shuffling mass; perhaps would have lingered till the hour struck, if there had not drifted to his memory the evening at Vallance's when Holt had declared this night to be impossible—and when Markham had "made it war." And, with that, he remembered also that Markham had rooms near by—in one of the turnings off Great Smith Street.

There was a light in the room that he knew for Markham's and it was only after he had rung that he wondered what had urged him to come. He was still wondering when the door opened and could think of no better explanation than "I saw you were up—by your light."

"If you'd passed five minutes ago," said Markham, as he led the way upstairs, "you wouldn't have seen any light. I'm only just back from the lab—and dining off biscuits and whisky."

"Is this making any difference to you, then?" Theodore asked. "I mean, in the way of work?"

Markham nodded as he poured out his visitor's whisky. "Yes, I'm serving the country—the military people have taken me over, lock and stock: with everyone else, apparently, who has ever done chemical research. I've been pretty hard at it the last few days, ever since the scare was serious. . . . And you—are you soldiering?"

"No," said Theodore and told him of the departmental prohibition.

"It mayn't make much difference in the end," said Markham. . . . "You see, I was right—the other evening."

"Yes," Theodore answered, "I believe that was why I came in. The crowd to-night reminded me of what you said at Vallance's—though I don't think I believed you then. . . . How long is it going to last?"

"God knows," said Markham, with his mouth full of biscuit. "We shall have had enough of it—both sides— before very long; but it's one thing to march into hell with your head up and another to find a way out. . . . There's only one thing I'm fairly certain about—I ought to have been strangled at birth."

Theodore stared at him, not sure he had caught the last words.

"You ought to——?"

"Yes—you heard me right. If the human animal must fight—and nothing seems to stop it—it should kill off its scientific men. Stamp out the race of 'em, forbid it to exist. . . . Holt was also right that evening, fundamentally. You can't combine the practice of science and the art of war; in the end, it's one or the other. We, I think, are going to prove that—very definitely."

"And when you've proved it—we stop fighting?"

Markham shrugged his shoulders, thrust aside his plate and filled his pipe.

"Curious, the failure to understand the influence on ourselves of what we make and use. We just make and use and damn the consequence. . . . When Lavoisier invented the chemical balance, did he stop to consider the possibilities of chemical action in combination with outbursts of human emotion? If he had . . . !"

In the silence that followed they heard the chiming of three-quarters—and there flashed inconsequently into Theodore's memory, a vision of himself, a small boy with his hand in his mother's, staring up, round-eyed, at Big Ben of London—while his mother taught him the words that were fitted to the chime.

Lord—through—this—hour
Be—Thou—our—guide,

So—by—Thy—power
No—foot—shall—slide.

. . . That, or something like that. . . . Odd, that he should remember them now—when for years he had not remembered. . . . "Lord—through—this—hour——"

He realized suddenly that Markham was speaking—in jerks, between pulls at his pipe. ". . . And the same with mechanics—not the engine but the engine plus humanity. Take young James Watt and his interest in the lid of a tea-kettle! In France, by the way, they tell the same story of Papin; but, so far as the rest of us are concerned it doesn't much matter who first watched the lid of a kettle with intelligence—the point is that somebody watched it and saw certain of its latent possibilities. Only its more immediate possibilities—and we may take it for granted that amongst those which he did not foresee were the most important. The industrial system—the drawing of men into crowds where they might feed the machine and be fed by it—the shrinkage of the world through the use of mechanical transport. That—the shrinkage—when we first saw it coming, we took to mean union of peoples and the clasping of distant hands—forgetting that it also meant the cutting of distant throats. . . . Yet it might have struck us that we are all potential combatants—and the only known method of preventing a fight is to keep the combatants apart! These odd, simple facts that we all of us know—and lose sight of . . . the drawing together of peoples has always meant the clashing of their interests . . . and so new hatreds. Inevitably new hatreds."

Theodore quoted: "'All men hate each other naturally.' . . . You believe that?"

"Of individuals, no—but of all communities, yes. Is there any form of the life collective that is capable of love for its fellow—for another community? Is there any church that will stand aside that another church may be advantaged? . . . You and I are civilized, as man and man; but collectively we are part of a life whose only standard and motive is self-interest, its own advantage . . . a beast-life, morally. If you understand that, you understand to-night . . . Which demands from us sacrifices, makes none itself. . . . That's as far as we have got in the mass."

Through the half-open window came the hum and murmur of the crowd that waited for the hour. . . . Theodore stirred restlessly, conscious of the unseen turning of countless faces to the clock—and aware, through the murmur, of the frenzied little beating of his watch. . . . He hesitated to look at it—and when he drew it out and said "Five minutes more," his voice sounded oddly in his ears.

"Five minutes," said Markham. . . . He laughed suddenly and pushed the bottle across the table. "Do you know where we are now—you and I and all of us? On the crest of the centuries. They've carried us a long roll upwards and now here we are—on top! In five more minutes—three hundred little seconds—we shall hear the crest curl over. . . . Meanwhile, have a drink!"

He checked himself and held up a finger. "Your watch is slow!"

The hum and murmur of the crowd had ceased and through silence unbroken came the prayer of the Westminster chime.

Lord—through—this—hour
Be—Thou—our—guide,
So—by—Thy—power
No—foot—shall—slide.

There was no other sound for the twelve booming strokes of the hour: it was only as the last beat quivered into silence that there broke the moving thunder of a multitude.

"Over!" said Markham. "Hear it crash? . . . Well, here's to the centuries—after all, they did the best they knew for us!"

V

The war-footing arrangements of the Distribution Office included a system of food control involving local supervision; hence provincial centres came suddenly into being, and to one of these—at York—Theodore Savage was dispatched at little more than an hour's notice on the morning after war was declared. He telephoned Phillida and they met at King's Cross and had ten hurried minutes on the platform; she was still eager and excited, bubbling over with the impulse to action—was hoping to start training for hospital work—had been promised an opening—she would tell him all about it when she wrote. Her excitement took the bitterness out of the parting—perhaps, in her need to give and serve, she was even proud that the sacrifice of parting was demanded of her. . . . The last he saw of her was a smiling face and a cheery little wave of the hand.

He made the journey to York with a carriageful of friendly and talkative folk who, in normal days, would have been strangers to him and to each other; as it was, they exchanged newspapers and optimistic views and grew suddenly near to each other in their common interest and resentment. . . . That was what war meant in those first stirring days—friendliness, good comradeship, the desire to give and serve, the thrill of unwonted excitement. . . . Looking back from after years it seemed to him that mankind, in those days, was finer and more gracious than he had ever known it—than he would ever know it again.

The first excitement over, he lived somewhat tediously at York between his office and dingily respectable lodgings; discovering very swiftly that, so far as he, Theodore Savage, was concerned, a state of hostilities meant the reverse of alarums and excursions. For him it was the strictest of official routine and the multiplication of formalities. His hours of liberty were fewer than in London, his duties more tiresome, his chief less easy to get on with; there was frequent overtime, and leave—which meant Phillida—was not even a distant possibility. For all his honest desire of service he was soon frankly bored by his work; its atmosphere of minute regularity and insistent detail was out of keeping with the tremor and uncertainty of war, and there was something æsthetically wrong about a fussy process of docketing and checking while nations were at death grips and the fate of a world in the balance. . . . His one personal satisfaction was the town, York itself—the walls, the Bars, and above all the Minster; he lodged near the Minster, could see it from his window, and its enduring dignity was a daily relief alike from the feverish perusal of war news, his landlady's colour-scheme and taste in furniture and the fidgety trifling of the office.

In the evening he read many newspapers and wrote long letters to Phillida; who also, he gathered, had discovered that war might be tedious. "We haven't any patients yet," she scribbled him in one of her later letters, "but, of course, I'm learning all sorts of things that will be useful later on, when we do get them. Bandaging and making beds—and then we attend lectures. It's rather dull waiting and bandaging each other for practice—but naturally I'm thankful that there aren't enough casualties to go round. Up to now the regular hospitals have taken all that there are—'temporaries' like us don't get even a look in. . . . The news is really splendid, isn't it?"

There were few casualties in the beginning because curiously little happened; Western Europe was removed from the actual storm-centre, and in England, after the first few days of alarmist rumours concerning invasion by air and sea, the war, for a time, settled down into a certain amount of precautionary rationing and a daily excitement in newspaper form—so much so that the timorous well-to-do, who had retired from London on the outbreak of hostilities, trickled back in increasing numbers. Hostilities, in the beginning, were local and comparatively ineffective; one of the results of the limitation of troops and armaments enforced by the constitution of the League was to give to the opening moves of the contest a character unprepared and amateurish. The aim, on either side, was to obtain time for effective preparation, to organize forces and resources; to train fighters and mobilize chemists, to convert factories, manufacture explosive and gas, and institute a system of co-operation between the strategy of far-flung allies. Hence, in the beginning, the conflict was partial and, as regards its strategy, hesitating; there were spasms of bloody incident which were deadly enough in themselves, but neither side cared to engage itself seriously before it had attained its full strength. . . . First blood was shed in a fashion that was frankly mediæval; the heady little democracy whose failure to establish a claim in the Court of Arbitration had been the immediate cause of the conflict, flung itself with all its half-civilized resources upon its neighbour and enemy, the victorious party to the suit. Between the two little communities was a treasured feud which had burst out periodically in defiance of courts and councils; and, control once removed, the border tribesmen gathered for the fray with all the enthusiasm of their rude forefathers, and raided each other's territory in bands armed with knives and revolvers. Their doings made spirited reading in the press in the early days of the war—before the generality of newspaper readers had even begun to realize that battles were no longer won by the shock of troops and that the root-principle of modern warfare was the use of the enemy civilian population as an auxiliary destructive force.

Certain states and races grasped the principle sooner than others, being marked out for early enlightenment by the accident of geographical position. In those not immediately affected, such as Britain, censorship on either side ruled out, as impossible for publication, the extent of the damage inflicted on allies, and the fact that it was not only in enemy countries that large masses of population, hunted out of cities by chemical warfare and the terror from above, had become nomadic and predatory. That, as the struggle grew fiercer, became, inevitably, the declared aim of the strategist; the exhaustion of the enemy by burdening him with a starving and nomadic population. War, once a matter of armies in the field, had resolved itself into an open and thorough-going effort to ruin enemy industry by setting his people on the run; to destroy enemy agriculture not only by incendiary devices—the so-called poison-fire—but by the secondary and even more potent agency of starving millions driven out to forage as they could. . . . The process, in the stilted phrase of the communiqué, was described as "displacement of population"; and displacement of population, not victory in the field, became the real military objective.

To the soldier, at least, it was evident very early in the struggle that the perfection of scientific destruction had entailed, of necessity, the indirect system of strategy associated with industrial warfare; displacement of population being no more than a natural development of the striker's method of attacking a government by starving the non-combatant community. The aim of the scientific soldier, like that of the soldier of the past, was to cut his enemy's communications, to intercept and hamper his supplies; and the obvious way to attain that end was by ruthless disorganization of industrial centres, by letting loose a famished industrial population to trample and devour his crops. Manufacturing districts, on either side, were rendered impossible to work in by making them impossible to live in; and from one crowded centre after another there streamed out squalid and panic-stricken herds, devouring the country as they fled. Seeking food, seeking refuge, turning this way or that; pursued by the terror overhead or imagining themselves pursued; and breaking, striving to separate, to make themselves small and invisible. . . . And, as air-fleets increased in strength and tactics were perfected—as one centre of industry after another went down and out—the process of disintegration was rapid. To the tentative and hesitating opening of the war had succeeded a fury of widespread destruction; and statesmen, rendered desperate by the sudden crumbling of their own people—the sudden lapse into primitive conditions—could hope for salvation only through a quicker process of "displacement" on the enemy side.

There were reasons, political and military, why the average British civilian, during the opening phases of the struggle, knew little of warfare beyond certain food restrictions, the news vouchsafed in the communiqués and the regulation comments thereon; the enemy forces which might have brought home to him the meaning of the term "displacement" were occupied at first with other and nearer antagonists. Hence continental Europe—and not Europe alone—was spotted with ulcers of spreading devastation before displacement was practised in England. There had been stirrings of uneasiness from time to time—of uneasiness and almost of wonder that the weapon she was using with deadly effect had not been turned against herself; but at the actual moment of invasion there was something like public confidence in a speedy end to the struggle—and the principal public grievance was the shortage and high price of groceries.

Whatever he forgot and confused in after days—and there were stretches of time that remained with him only as a blur—Theodore remembered very clearly every detail and event of the night when disaster began. Young Hewlett's voice as he announced disaster—and what he, Theodore, was doing when the boy rapped on the window. Not only what happened, but his mood when the interruption came and the causes of it; he had suffered an irritating day at the office, crossed swords with a self-important chief and been openly snubbed for his pains. As a result, his landlady's evening grumble on the difficulties of war-time housekeeping seemed longer and less bearable than usual, and he was still out of tune with the world in general when he sat down to write to Phillida. He remembered phrases of the letter—never posted— wherein he worked off his irritation. "I got into trouble to-day through thinking of you when I was supposed to be occupied with indents. You are responsible, Blessed Girl, for several most horrible muckers, affecting the service of the country. . . . Your empty hospital don't want you and my empty-headed boss don't want me—oh, lady mine, if I could only make him happy by sacking myself and catching the next train to London!" . . . And so on and so on. . . .

It was late, nearing midnight, when he finished his letter and, for want of other occupation, turned back to a half-read evening paper; the communiqués were meagre, but there was a leading article pointing out the inevitable effect of displacement on the enemy's resources and morale, and he waded through its comfortable optimism.

As he laid aside the paper he realized how sleepy he was and rose yawning; he was on his way to the door, with intent to turn in, when the rapping on the window halted him. He pulled aside the blind and saw a face against the glass—pressed close, with a flattened white nose.

"Who's that?" he asked, pushing up the window. It was Hewlett, one of his juniors at the office, out of breath with running and excitement.

"I say, Savage, come along out. There's no end going on—fires, the whole sky's red. They've come over at last and no mistake. Crashaw and I have been watching 'em and I thought you'd like to have a look. It's worth seeing—we're just along there, on the wall. Hurry up!"

The boy was dancing with eagerness to get back and Theodore had to run to keep up with him. He and Crashaw, Hewlett explained in gasps, had spent the evening in a billiard-room; it was on their way back to their diggings that they had noticed sudden lights in the sky—sort of flashes—and gone up on the wall to see better. . . . No, it wasn't only searchlights—you could see them too—sudden flashes and the sky all red. Fires—to the south. It was the real thing, no doubt about that—and the only wonder was why they hadn't come before. . . . At the head of the steps leading up to the wall were three or four figures with their heads all turned one way; and as Hewlett, mounting first, called "Still going on?" another voice called back, "Rather!"

They stood on the broad, flat wall and watched—in a chill little wind. The skyline to the south and south-west was reddened with a glow that flickered and wavered spasmodically and, as Hewlett had said, there were flashes—the bursting of explosive or star-shells. Also there were moments when the reddened skyline throbbed suddenly in places, grew vividly golden and sent out long fiery streamers. . . . They guessed at direction and wondered how far off; the wind was blowing sharply from the north, towards the glow; hence it carried sound away from them and it was only now and then that they caught more than a mutter and rumble.

As the minutes drew out the news spread through the town and the watchers on the wall increased in numbers; not only men but women, roused from bed, who greeted the flares with shrill, excited "Oh's" and put ceaseless questions to their men folk. Young Hewlett, at Theodore's elbow, gave himself up to frank interest in his first sight of war; justifying a cheerfulness that amounted to enthusiasm by explaining at intervals that he guessed our fellows were giving 'em what for and by this time they were sorry they'd come. . . . Once a shawled woman demanded tartly why they didn't leave off, then, if they'd had enough? Whereat Hewlett, unable to think of an answer, pretended not to hear and moved away.

Of his own sensations while he watched from the wall Theodore remembered little save the bodily sensation of chill; he saw himself standing with his back to the wind, his shoulders hunched and the collar of his coat turned up. The murmur of hushed voices remained with him and odd snatches of fragmentary talk; there was the woman who persisted uneasily, "But you can't 'ear 'em coming with these 'ere silent engines—why, they might be right over us naow!" And the man who answered her gruffly with "You'd jolly well know if they were!" . . . And perpetual conjecture as to distance and direction of the glow; disputes between those who asserted that over there was Leeds, and those who scoffed contemptuously at the idea—arguing that, if Leeds were the centre of disturbance, the guns would have sounded much nearer. . . . Petty talk, he remembered, and plainly enough—but not how much he feared or foresaw. He must have been anxious, uneasy, or he would not have stood for long hours in the chill of the wind; but his definite impressions were only of scattered, for the most part uneducated, talk, of silhouetted figures that shifted and grouped, of turning his eyes from the lurid skyline to the shadowy rock that in daylight was the mass of the cathedral. . . . In the end sheer craving for warmth drove him in; leaving Hewlett and Crashaw deaf to his reminder that the office expected them at nine.

With the morning came news and—more plentifully— rumour; also, the wind having dropped, a persistent thunder from the south. Industrial Yorkshire, it was clear, was being subjected to that process of human displacement which, so far, it had looked on as an item in the daily communiqué; the attack, moreover, was an attack in force, since the invaders did not find it needful to desist with the passing of darkness. Rumour, in the absence of official intelligence, invented an enveloping air-fleet which should cut them off from their base; and meanwhile the thunder continued. . . .

This much, at least, was shortly official and certain: nearly all rail, road and postal communication to the south was cut off—trains had ceased to run Londonwards and ordinary traffic on the highways was held up at barriers and turned back. Only military cars used the roads—and returned to add their reports to those brought in by air-scouts; but as a rule the information they furnished was for official enlightenment only, and it was not till the refugees arrived in numbers that the full meaning of displacement was made clear to the ordinary man.

It was after the second red night that the refugees appeared in their thousands—a horde of human rats driven out of their holes by terror, by fire and by gas. Whatever their status and possessions in the life of peace, they came with few exceptions on foot; as roads, like railways, were a target for the airman, the highway was avoided for the by-path or the open field, and the flight from every panic-stricken centre could be traced by long wastes of trampled crops. There were those who, terrified beyond bearing by the crash of masonry and long trembling underground, saw safety only in the roofless open, refused to enter houses and persisted in huddling in fields—unafraid, as yet, of the so-called poison-fire which had licked up the crops in Holderness and the corn-growing district round Pontefract. . . . Leeds, for a day or two, was hardly touched; but with the outpouring of fugitives from Dewsbury, Wakefield, Halifax and Bradford, Leeds also began to vomit her terrified multitudes. A wave of vagrant destitution rushed suddenly and blindly northward—anywhere away from the ruin of explosive, the flames and death by suffocation; while authority strove vainly to control and direct the torrent of overpowering misery.

It was in the early morning that the torrent reached York and rolled through it; overwhelming the charity, private and public, that at first made efforts to cope with the rush of misery. Theodore's room for a time was given up to a man with bandaged eyes and puffed face whom his wife had led blindfold from Castleford. The man himself sat dumb and suffering, breathing heavily through blistered lips; the woman raged vulgarly against the Government which had neglected to supply them with gas-masks, to have the place properly defended, to warn people! "The bloody fools ought to have known what was coming and if her man was blinded for the rest of his life it was all the fault of this 'ere Government that never troubled its blasted 'ead as long as it drew its money." . . . That was in the beginning, before the flood of misery had swollen so high that even the kindliest shrank from its squalid menace; and Theodore, because it was the first he heard, remembered her story when he had forgotten others more piteous.

Before midday there was only one problem for local authority, civil and military—the disposal of displaced population; that is to say, the herding of vagrants that could not all be sheltered, that could not all be fed, that blackened fields, choked streets, drove onward and sank from exhaustion. The railway line to the north was still clear and, in obedience to wireless instructions from London, trains packed with refugees were sent off to the north, with the aim of relieving the pressure on local resources. Disorganization of transport increased the difficulty of food supply and even on the first day of panic and migration the agricultural community were raising a cry of alarm. Blind terror and hunger between them wrought havoc; fields were trampled and fugitives were plundering already—would plunder more recklessly to-morrow.

All day, all night, displaced humanity came stumbling in panic from the south and south-west; spreading news of the torment it had fled from, the dead it had left and the worse than dead who still crouched in an inferno whence they could not summon courage to fly. The railways could not deal with a tithe of the number who clamoured to be carried to the north, into safety; by the first evening the town was well-nigh eaten out, and householders, hardening their hearts against misery, were bolting themselves in, for fear of misery grown desperate. While out in the country farmers stabled their live-stock and kept ceaseless watch against the hungry.

All day the approaches to the station were besieged by those who hoped for a train; and, on the second night of the invasion, Theodore, sent by his chief with a message to the military transport officer, fought his way through a solid crowd on the platform—a crowd excluded from a train that was packed and struggling with humanity. A crowd that was squalid, unreasoning and blindly selfish; intent only on flight and safety—and some of it brutally intent. There were scuffles with porters and soldiers who refused to open locked doors, angry hootings and wild swayings backward and forward as the train moved out of the station; Theodore's efforts to make his way to the station-master's office were held to be indicative of a desire to travel by the next train and he was buffeted aside without mercy. There was something in the brute mass of terror that sickened him—a suggestion already of the bestial, the instinctive, the un-human.

The transport officer looked up at him with tired, angry eyes and demanded what the hell he wanted? . . . Whereat Theodore handed him a typewritten note from a punctilious chief and explained that they had tried to get through on the telephone, either to him or the station-master, but——

"I should rather think not," said the transport officer rudely. "We've both of us got more important things to worry about than little Distribution people. The telephone clerk did bring me some idiotic message or other, but I told him I didn't want to hear it."

He glanced at the typewritten note—then glared at it—and went off into a cackle of laughter; which finally tailed into blasphemy coupled with obscene abuse.

"Seen this?" he asked when he had sworn himself out. "Well, at any rate you know what it's about. The——has sent for particulars of to-morrow's refugee train service—wants to know the number and capacity of trains to be dispatched to Newcastle-on-Tyne. Wants to enter it in duplicate, I suppose—and make lots and lots and lots of carbon copies. God in Heaven!"—and again he sputtered into blasphemy. . . . "Well, I needn't bother to write down the answer; even if you've no more sense than he has, you'll be able to remember it all right. It's nil to both questions; nil trains to Newcastle, nil capacity. So that's that! . . . What's more—if it's any satisfaction to your darned-fool boss to know it—we haven't been sending any trains to Newcastle all day."

"But I thought," began Theodore—wondering if the man were drunk? He was, more than slightly—having fought for two days with panic-stricken devils and helped himself through with much whisky; but, drunk or not, he was sure of his facts and rapped them out with authority.

"Not to Newcastle. The first two or three got as far as Darlington—this morning. There they were pulled up. Then it was Northallerton—now we send 'em off to Thirsk and leave the people there to deal with 'em. You bet they'll send 'em further if they can—you don't suppose they want to be eaten out, any more than we do. But, for all I know, they're getting 'em in from the other side."

"The other side?" Theodore repeated. "What do you mean?" Whereat the transport officer, grown suddenly uncommunicative, leaned back in his chair and whistled.

"That's all I can tell you," he vouchsafed at length. "Trains haven't run beyond Darlington since yesterday. I conclude H.Q. knows the reason, but they haven't imparted it to me—I've only had my orders. It isn't our business if the trains get stopped so long as we send 'em off—and we're sending 'em and asking no questions."

"Do you mean," Theodore stammered, "that—this—is going on up north?"

"What do you think?" said the transport officer. "It's the usual trick, isn't it? . . . Start 'em running from two sides at once—don't let 'em settle, send 'em backwards and forwards, keep 'em going! . . . We've played it often enough on them—now we're getting a bit of our own back. . . . However, I've no official information. You know just as much as I do."

"But," Theodore persisted, "the people coming through from the north. What do they say—they must know?"

"There aren't any people coming through," said the other grimly. "Military order since this morning—no passenger traffic from the north runs this side of Thirsk. We've got enough of our own, haven't we? . . . All I say is—God help Thirsk and especially God help the station-master!"

He straightened himself suddenly and grabbed at the papers on his table.

"Now, you've got what the damn fool sent you for—and I'm trying to make out my report."

As Theodore fought his way out of the station and the crowd that seethed round it, he had an intolerable sense of being imprisoned between two fires. If he could see far enough to the north—to Durham and the Tyneside—there would be another hot, throbbing horizon and another stream of human destitution pouring lamentably into the night. . . . And, between the two fires, the two streams were meeting—turning back upon themselves, intermingling . . . in blind and agonized obedience to the order to "keep 'em going!" . . . What happened when a train was halted by signal and the thronged misery inside it learned that here, without forethought or provision made, its flight must come to an end? At Thirsk, Northallerton, by the wayside, anywhere, in darkness? . . . A thin sweep of rain was driving down the street, and he fancied wretched voices calling through darkness, through rain. Asking what, in God's name, was to become of them and where, in God's name, they were to go? . . . And the overworked officials who could give no answer, seeking only to be rid of the massed and dreadful helplessness that cumbered the ground on which it trod! . . . Displacement of population—the daily, stilted phrase—had become to him a raw and livid fact and he stood amazed at the limits of his own imagination. Day after day he had read the phrase, been familiar with it; yet, so far, the horror had been words to him. Now the daily, stilted phrase was translated, comprehensible: "Don't let 'em settle—keep 'em going."

Back at the office, he discovered that his errand to the station had been superfluous; his chief, the man of precedent, order and many carbon copies, was staring, haggard and bewildered, at a typewritten document signed by the military commandant. . . . And obtaining, incidentally, his first glimpse into a world till now unthinkable—where precedent was not, where reference was useless and order had ceased to exist.

VI

That night ended Theodore's life as a clerk in the Civil Service. The confusion consequent on the breakdown of transport had left of the Distribution system but a paralysed mockery, a name without functions attached to it; and with morning Theodore and his able-bodied fellows were impressed into a special constabulary, hastily organized as a weapon against vagrancy grown desperate and riotous. They were armleted, put through a hurried course of instruction, furnished with revolvers or rifles and told to shoot plunderers at sight.

No system of improvised rationing could satisfy even the elementary needs of the hundreds of thousands who swept hither and thither, as panic seized or the invader drove them; hence military authority, in self-preservation, turned perforce on the growing menace of fugitive and destitute humanity. Order, so long as the semblance of it lasted, strove to protect and maintain the supplies of the fighting forces; which entailed, inevitably, the leaving to the fate of their own devices of the famished useless, the horde of devouring mouths. Interruption of transport meant entire dependence on local food stuffs; and, as stocks grew lower and plundering increased, provisions were seized by the military. . . . Theodore, in the first hours of his new duty, helped to load an armed lorry with the contents of a grocer's shop and fight it through the streets of York. There was an ugly rush as the driver started his engine; men who had been foodless for days had watched, in sullen craving, while the shop was emptied of its treasure of sacks and tins; and when the engine buzzed a child wailed miserably, a woman shrieked "Don't let them, don't let them!" and the whole pack snarled and surged forward. Wolfish white faces showed at the tailboard and before the car drew clear her escort had used their revolvers. Theodore, not yet hardened to shooting, seized the nearest missile, a tin of meat, and hurled it into one of the faces; when they drew away three or four of the pack were tearing at each other for the treasure contained in the tin.

He noticed, as the days went by, how quickly he slipped from the outlook and habits of civilized man and adopted those of the primitive, even of the animal. It was not only that he was suspicious of every man, careful in approach, on the alert and ready for violence; he learned, like the animal, to be indifferent to the suffering that did not concern him. Violence, when it did not affect him directly, was a noise in the distance—no more; and as swiftly as he became inured to bloodshed he grew hardened to the sight of misery. At first he had sickened when he ate his rations at the thought of a million-fold suffering that starved while he filled his stomach; later, as order's representative, he herded and hustled a massed starvation without scruple, driving it away when it grouped itself threateningly, shooting when it promised to give trouble to authority, and looking upon death, itself, indifferently.

It amazed him, looking back, to realize the swiftness with which ordered society had crumbled; laws, systems, habits of body and mind—they had gone, leaving nothing but animal fear and the animal need to be fed. Within little more than a week of the night when young Hewlett had called him to watch the red flashes and the glare in the sky, there remained of the fabric of order built up through the centuries very little but a military force that was fighting on two sides—against inward disorder and alien attack—and struggling to maintain itself alive. Automatically, inevitably—under pressure of starvation, blind vagrancy and terror—that which had once been a people, an administrative whole, was relapsing into a tribal separatism, the last barrier against nomadic anarchy. . . . As famished destitution overran the country, localities not yet destitute tried systematically and desperately to shut out the vagrant and defended what was left to them by force. Countrymen beat off the human plague that devoured their substance and trampled their crops underfoot; barriers were erected that no stranger might pass and bloody little skirmishes were frequent at the outskirts of villages. As bread grew scarcer and more precious, the penalties on those who stole it were increasingly savage; tribal justice—lynch law—took the place of petty sessions and assize, and plunderers, even suspected plunderers, were strung up to trees and their bodies left dangling as a warning. . . . And a day or two later, it might be, the poison-fire swept through the fields and devoured the homes of those who had executed tribal justice; or a horde of destitution, too strong to be denied, drove them out; and, homeless in their turn, they swelled the tide of plunderers and vagrants. . . . Man, with bewildering rapidity, was slipping through the stages whereby, through the striving of long generations, he had raised himself from primitive barbarism and the law that he shares with the brute.

Very steadily the process of displacement continued. On most nights, in one direction or another, there were sudden outbursts of light—the glare of explosion or burning buildings or the greenish-blue reflection of the poison-fire. The silent engine gave no warning of its coming, and the first announcement of danger was the bursting of gas-shell and high explosive, or the sudden vivid pallor of the poison-fire as it ran before the wind and swept along dry fields and hedgerows. Where it swept it left not only long tracts of burned crop and black skeleton trees, but, often enough, the charred bodies of the homeless whom its rush had outpaced and overtaken. . . . Sudden and unreasoning panic was frequent—wild rushes from imaginary threats—and there were many towns which, when their turn came, were shells and empty buildings only; dead towns, whence the inhabitants had already fled in a body. York had been standing all but silent for days when an enemy swooped down to destroy it and Theodore, guarding military stores in a camp on the Ripon road, looked his last on the towers of the Minster, magnificent against a sea of flame. Death, in humanity, had ceased to move him greatly; but he turned away his head from the death of high human achievement.

For the first few days of disaster there was a certain amount of news, or what passed for news, from the outside world; in districts yet untouched and not wholly panic-stricken, local journals struggled out and communiqués—true or false—were published by the military authorities. But with the rapid growth of the life nomadic, the herding and driving to and fro, with the consequent absence of centres for the dissemination of news or information, the outside world withdrew to a distance and veiled itself in silence unbroken. With the disappearance of the newspaper there was left only rumour, and rumour was always current—sometimes hopeful, sometimes dreadful, always wild; to-day, Peace was coming, a treaty all but signed—and to-morrow London was in ruins. . . . No one knew for certain what was happening out of eyeshot, or could more than guess how far devastation extended. This alone was a certainty; that in every direction that a man might turn, he met those who were flying from destruction, threatened or actual; and that night after night and day after day, humanity crouched before the science itself had perfected. . . . Sometimes there were visible encounters in the air, contending squadrons that chased, manœuvred and gave battle; but the invaders, driven off, returned again and the process of displacement continued. And, with every hour of its continuance, the death-roll grew longer, uncounted; and men, who had struggled to retain a hold on their humanity and the life civilized, gave up the struggle, became predatory beasts and fought with each other for the means to keep life in their bodies.

In after years Theodore tried vainly to remember how long he was quartered in the camp on the Ripon road—whether it was weeks or a matter of days only. Then or later he lost all sense of time, retaining only a memory of happenings, of events that followed each other and connecting them roughly with the seasons—frosty mornings, wet and wind or summer heat. There were the nights when York flamed and the days when thick smoke hung over it; and the morning when aeroplanes fought overhead and two crashed within a mile of the camp. There was the night of pitched battle with a rabble of the starving, grown desperate, which rushed the guard suddenly out of the darkness and beat and hacked at the doors of the sheds which contained the hoarded treasure of food. Theodore, with every other man in the camp, was turned out hastily to do battle with the horde of invaders—to shoot into the mass of them and drive them back to their starvation. In the end the rush was stemmed and the camp cleared of the mob; but there was a hideous five minutes of shots and knife-thrusts and hand-to-hand struggling before the final stampede. Even after the stampede the menace was not at an end; when the sun rose it showed to the watchers in the camp a sullen rabble that lingered not a field's breadth distant—a couple of hundred wolfish men and women who could not tear themselves away from the neighbourhood of food, who glared covetously and took hopeless counsel together till the order to charge them was given and they broke and fled, spitting back hatred.

After that, the night guard was doubled and the commanding officer applied in haste for reinforcements; barbed wire entanglements were stretched round the camp and orders were given to disperse any crowd that assembled and lingered in the neighbourhood. Behind their entanglements and line of sentries the little garrison lived as on an island in the flood of anarchy and ruin—a remnant of order, defending itself against chaos. And, for all the discipline with which they faced anarchy and the ruthlessness with which they beat back chaos, they knew (so often as they dared to think) that the time might be at hand—must be at hand, if no deliverance came— when they, every man of them, would be swept from their island to the common fate and become as the creatures, scarce human, who crawled to them for food and were refused. When darkness fell and flames showed red on the horizon, they would wonder how long before their own turn came—and be thankful for the lightening in the east; and as each convoy of lorries drove up to remove supplies from their fast dwindling stores, they would scan the faces of men who were ignorant and helpless as themselves to see if they were bearers of good news. . . . And the news was always their own news repeated; of ruin and burning, of famine and the threat of the famished. No message—save stereotyped military orders—from that outside world whence alone they could hope for salvation.

There remained with Theodore to the end of his days the dreadful memory of the women. At the beginning—just at the beginning—of disaster, authority had connived at a certain amount of charitable diversion of military stores for the benefit of women and children; but as supplies dwindled and destroying hordes of vagrants multiplied, the tacit permission was withdrawn. The soldier, the instrument of order, unfed was an instrument of order no longer; discipline was discipline for so long only as it obtained the necessities of life, and troops whose rations failed them in the end ceased to be troops and swelled the flood of vagrant and destitute anarchy. The useless mouth was the weapon of the enemy; and authority hardened its heart perforce against the crying of the useless mouth.

Once a score or so of women, with a tall, frantic girl as their leader, stood for hours at the edge of the wire entanglement and called on the soldiers to shoot—if they would not feed them, to shoot. Then, receiving only silence as answer, the tall girl cried out that, by God, the soldiers should be forced to shoot! and led her companions—some cumbered with children—to tear and hurl themselves across the stretch of barbed and twisted wire. As they scrambled over, bleeding, crying and their clothes in rags, they were seized by the wrists and hustled to the gate of the camp—some limp and effortless, others kicking and writhing to get free. When the gate was closed and barred on them they beat on it—then lay about wretchedly . . . and at last shambled wretchedly away. . . .

More dreadful even than the women who dragged with them children they could not feed, were those who sought to bribe the possessors of food with the remnant of their feminine attractions; who eyed themselves anxiously in streams, pulled their sodden clothes into a semblance of jauntiness and made piteous attempts at flirtation. Money being worthless, since it could buy neither safety nor food, the price for those who traded their bodies was paid in a hunk of bread or meat. . . . Those women suffered most who had no man of their own to forage and fend for them, and were no longer young enough for other men to look on with pleasure. They—as humanity fell to sheer wolfishness and the right of the strongest—were beaten back and thrust aside when it came to the sharing-out of spoil.

He remembered very clearly a day when news that was authentic reached them from the outside world; an aeroplane came down with engine-trouble in a field on the edge of the camp, and the haggard-faced pilot, beset with breathless questions, laughed roughly when they asked him of London—how lately he had been there, what was happening? "Oh yes, I was over it a day or two ago. You're no worse off than they are down south—London's been on the run for days." He turned back to his engine and whistled tunelessly through the silence that had fallen on his hearers. . . . Theodore said it over slowly to himself, "London's been on the run for days." If so—if so—then what, in God's name, of Phillida?

Hitherto he had fought back his dread for Phillida, denying to himself, as he denied to others, the rumour that disaster was widespread and general, and insisting that she, at least, was safe. If there was one thing intolerable, one thing that could not be, it was Phillida vagrant, Phillida starving—his dainty lady bedraggled and grovelling for her bread. . . . like the haggard women who had beaten with their hands on the gate. . . .

"It must stop," he choked suddenly, "it must stop—it can't go on!"

The pilot broke off from his whistling to stare at the distorted face.

"No," he said grimly, "it can't go on. What's more, it's stopping, by degrees—stopping itself; you mayn't have noticed it yet, but we do. Taking 'em all round they're leaving off, not coming as thick as they did. And"—his mouth twisted ironically—"we're leaving off and for the same reason."

"The same reason?" someone echoed him.

"Because we can't go on. . . . You don't expect us to carry on long in this, do you?" He shrugged and jerked his head towards a smoke cloud on the western skyline. "That's what ran us—gone up in smoke. Food and factories and transport and Lord knows what beside. The things that ran us and kept us going . . . We're living on our own fat now—what there is of it—and so are the people on the other side. We can just keep going as long as it lasts; but it's getting precious short now, and when we've finished it—when there's no fat left! . . ." He laughed unpleasantly and stared at the rolling smoke cloud.

Someone else asked him about the rumour ever-current of negotiation—whether there was truth in it, whether he had heard anything?

"Much what you've heard," he said, and shrugged his shoulders. "There's talk—there always is—plenty of it; but I don't suppose I know any more than you do. . . . It stands to reason that someone must be trying to put an end to it—but who's trying to patch it up with who? . . . And what is there left to patch? Lord knows! They say the real trouble is that when governments have gone there's no one to negotiate with. No responsible authority—sometimes no authority at all. Nothing to get hold of. You can't make terms with rabble; you can't even find out what it wants—and it's rabble now, here, there, and everywhere. When there's nothing else left, how do you get hold of it, treat with it? Who makes terms, who signs, who orders? . . . Meanwhile, we go on till we're told to stop—those of us that are left. . . . And I suppose they're doing much the same—keeping on because they don't know how to stop."

Theodore asked what he meant when he spoke of "no government." "You can't mean it literally? You can't mean . . . ?"

"Why not?" said the pilot. "Is there any here?"—and jerked his head, this time towards the road. Its long white ribbon was spotted with groups and single figures of vagrants—scarecrow vagrants—crawling onward they knew not whither.

"See that," he said, "see that—does anyone govern it? Make rules for it, defend it, keep it alive? . . . And that's everywhere."

Someone whispered back "Everywhere" under his breath; the rest stared in silence at the spotted white ribbon of road.

"You can't mean . . . ?" said Theodore again.

The airman shrugged his shoulders and laughed roughly.

"I believe," he said, "there are still some wretched people who call themselves a government, try to be a government—at least, there were the other day. . . . Sometimes I wonder *how* they try, what they say to each other—poor devils! How they look when the heads of what used to be departments bring them in the day's report? Can't you imagine their silly, ghastly faces? . . . Even if they're still in existence, what in God's name can they do—except let us go on killing each other in the hope that something may turn up. If they give orders, sign papers, make laws, does anyone listen, pay any attention? Does it make any difference to *that*?" Again he jerked his head towards the road, and in the word as in the gesture was loathing, fear and contempt. "And in other parts of what used to be the civilized world—where this sort of hell has been going on longer—what do you suppose is happening?"

No one answered; he laughed again roughly, as if he were contemptuous of their hopes, and a man beside Theodore—a corporal—swung round on him, white-faced and snarling.

"Damn you! . . . I've got a girl. . . . I've got a girl! . . ."

He choked, moved away and stood rigid, staring at the road.

Theodore heard himself asking, "If there isn't any government—what is there?"

"What's left of the army," said the other, "that's all that hangs together. Bits of it, here and there—getting smaller, losing touch with the other bits; hanging on to its rations—what's left of 'em. . . . And we hold together just as long as we can fight back the rabble; not an hour, not a minute longer! When we've gnawed our way through the last of our rations—what then? . . . You may do what you like, but I'm keeping a shot for myself. Whether we're through with it or whether we're not. Just stopping fighting won't clear up this mess. . . . And I'll die—what I am. Not rabble!"

Whether after days or whether after weeks, there came a time when they ceased to have dealings with the world beyond their wire defences; when the store-sheds in the camp were all but emptied of their hoard of foodstuffs and such military authority as might still exist took no further interest in the doings of a useless garrison. Orders and communications, once frequent, grew fewer, and finally, as military authority crumbled, they were left to isolation, to their own defence and devices. Since no man any longer had need of them, they were cut off from intercourse with those other remnants of the life disciplined whence lorries had once arrived in search of rations; separated from such other bands of their fellows as still held together, they were no longer part of an army, were nothing but a band of armed men. Though their own daily rations were cut down to the barest necessities of life, there was little grumbling, since even the dullest knew the reason; as the airman had told them, they were living on their own fat, for so long as their own fat lasted. For all their isolation, their fears and daily perils kept them disciplined; they held together, obeyed orders and kept watch, not because they still felt themselves part of a nation or a military force, but because there remained in their common keeping the means to support bare life. It was not loyalty or patriotism, but the sense of their common danger, their common need of defence against the famished world outside their camp, that kept them comrades, obedient to a measure of discipline, and made them still a community.

There had been altercation of the fiercest before they were left to themselves—when lorries drove up for food which was refused them, on the ground that the camp had not sufficient for its own needs. Disputes at the refusal were furious and violent; men, driven out forcibly, went off shouting threats that they would come back and take what was denied them—would bring their machine-guns and take it. Those who yet had the wherewithal to keep life in their bodies knew the necessity that prompted the threat and lived thenceforth in a state of siege against men who had once been their comrades. With the giving out of military supplies and the consequent breaking of the bonds of discipline, bands of soldiers, scouring the countryside, were an added terror to their fellow-vagrants and, so long as their ammunition lasted, fared better than starvation unarmed. . . . If central authority existed it gave no sign; while military force that had once been united—an army—dissolved into its primitive elements: tribes of armed men, held together by their fear of a common enemy. In the wreck of civilization, of its systems, institutions and polity, there endured longest that form of order which had first evolved from the chaos of barbarism—the disciplined strength of the soldier. . . . A people retracing its progress from chaos retraced it step by step.

VII

The end of civilization came to Theodore Savage and his fellows as it had come to uncounted thousands.

There had been a still warm day with a haze on it—he judged it early autumn or perhaps late summer; for the rest, like any other day in the camp routine—of watchfulness, of scanning the sky and the distance, of the passing of vagabond starvation, of an evil smell drifting with the lazy air from the dead who lay unburied where they fell. Before nightfall the haze was lifted by a cold little wind from the east; and soon after darkness a moon at the full cast white, merciless light and black shadow.

Theodore was asleep when the alarm was given—by a shout at the door of his hut. One of ten or a dozen, aroused like himself, he grabbed at his rifle as he stumbled to his feet; believing in the first hurried moment of waking that he was called to drive back yet another night onslaught of the starving enemy without. He ran out of the hut into a strong, pallid glare that wavered. . . . A stretch of gorse and bramble-patch two hundred yards away was alight, burning lividly, and further off the same bluish flame was running like a wave across a field. Enemy aeroplanes were dropping their fire-bombs—here and there, flash on flash, of pale, inextinguishable flame.

It was scarcely five minutes from the time he had been roused before the camp and its garrison had ceased to exist as a community, and Theodore Savage and his living comrades were vagabonds on the face of the earth. The gorse and bramble-patch lay to the eastward and the wind was blowing from the east; the flames rushed triumphantly at a black clump of fir trees—great torches that lit up the neighbourhood. The guiding hand in the terror overhead had a mark laid ready for his aim; the camp, with its camouflaged huts and sheds, seen plainly as in broadest daylight. His next bomb burst in the middle of the camp blowing half-a-score of soldiers into bloody fragments and firing the nearest wooden building. While it burned, the terror overhead struck again and again—then stooped to its helpless quarry and turned a machine-gun on men in trenches and men running hither and thither in search of a darkness that might cover them. . . . That, for Theodore Savage, was the ending of civilization.

With the crash of the first explosion he cowered instinctively and pressed himself against the wall of the nearest shed; the flames, rushing upward, showed him others cowering like himself, all striving to obliterate themselves, to shrink, to deny their humanity. Even in his extremity of bodily fear he was conscious of merciless humiliation; the machine-gun crackled at scurrying little creatures that once were men and that now were but impotent flesh at the mercy of mechanical perfection. . . . Mechanical perfection, the work of men's hands, soared over its creators, spat down at their helplessness and defaced them; they cringed in corners till it found them out and ran from it screaming, without power to strike back at the invisible beast that pursued them. Without power even to surrender and yield to its mercy; they could only hate impotently—and run. . . .

As they ran they broke instinctively—avoiding each other, since a group made a mark for a gunner. Theodore, when he dared cower no longer, rushed with a dozen through the gate of the camp but, once outside it, they scattered right and left and there was no one near him when his flight ended with a stumble. He stayed where he had fallen, a good mile from the camp, in the blessed shadow of a hedgerow; he crept close to it and lay in the blackness of the shadow, breathing great sobs and trembling—crouching in dank grass and peering through the leafage at the distant furnace he had fled from. The crackling of machine-guns had ceased, but here and there, for miles around were stretches of flame running rapidly before a dry wind. Half a mile away an orchard was blazing with hayricks; and he drew a long sigh of relief when another flare leaped up—further off. That was miles away, that last one; they were going, thank God they were going! . . . He waited to make sure—half an hour or more—then stumbled back in search of his companions; through fields on to the road that led past what once had been the camp.

On his way he met others, dark figures creeping back like himself; by degrees a score or so gathered in the road-way and stood in little groups, some muttering, some silent, as they watched the flames burn themselves out. There were bodies lying in the road and beside it—men shot from above as they ran; and the living turned them over to look at their distorted faces. . . . No one was in authority; their commanding officer had been killed outright by the bursting of the first bomb, one of the subalterns lay huddled in the roadway, just breathing. So much they knew. . . . In the beginning there was relief that they had come through alive; but, with the passing of the first instinct of relief, came understanding of the meaning of being alive. . . . The breath in their bodies, the knowledge that they still walked the earth: and for the rest, vagrancy and beast-right—the right of the strongest to live!

They took counsel together as the night crept over them and—because there was nothing else to do—planned to search the charred ruin as the fire died out, in the hope of salvage from the camp. They counted such few, odd possessions as remained to them: cartridge belts, rifles thrown away in flight and then picked up in the road, the contents of their pockets—no more. . . . In the end, for the most part, they slept the dead sleep of exhaustion till morning—to wake with cold rain on their faces.

The rain, for all its wretchedness to men without shelter, was so far their friend that it beat down the flames on the smouldering timbers which were all that remained of their fortress and rock of defence. They burrowed feverishly among the black wreckage of their store-sheds, blistering and burning their fingers by too eager handling of logs that still flickered, unearthing, now and then, some scrap of charred meat but, for the most part, nothing but lumps of molten metal that had once been the tins containing food. In their pressing anxiety to avert the peril of hunger they were heedless of a peril yet greater; their search had attracted the attention of others—scarecrow vagrants, the rabble of the roads, who saw them from a distance and came hurrying in the hope of treasure-trove. The first single spies retreated at the order of superior and disciplined numbers; but with time their own numbers were swollen by those who halted at the rumour of food, and there hovered round the searchers a shifting, snarling, envious crowd that drew gradually nearer till faced with the threat of pointed rifles. Even that only stayed it for a little—and, spurred on by hunger, imagining riches where none existed, it rushed suddenly forward in a mob that might not be held.

Those who had rifles fired at it and men in the foremost ranks went down, unheeded in the rush of their fellows; those who might have hesitated were thrust forward by the frantic need behind, and the torrent of misery broke against the little group of soldiers in a tumult of grappling and screeching. Women, like men, asserted their beast-right to food—when sticks and knives failed them, asserted it with claws and teeth; unhuman creatures, with eyes distended and wide, yelling mouths, went down with their fingers at each other's throats, their nails in each other's flesh. . . . Theodore clubbed a length of burnt wood and struck out . . . saw a man drop with a broken, bloody face and a woman back from him shrieking . . . then was gripped from behind, with an arm round his neck, and went down. . . . The famished creatures fought above his body and beat out his senses with their feet.

When life came back to him the sun was very low in the west. In his head little hammers beat intolerably and all his strained body ached with bruises as he raised himself, slowly and groaning, and leaned on an arm to look round. He lay much where he had fallen, but the soldiers, the crowd of human beasts, had vanished; the bare stretch of camp, still smoking in places, was silent and almost deserted. Two or three bending and intent figures were hovering round the charred masses of wreckage—moving slowly, stopping often, peering as they walked and thrusting their hands into the ashes, in the hope of some fragment that those who searched before them had missed. A woman lay face downwards with her dead arm flung across his feet; further off were other bodies—which the searchers passed without notice. Three or four were in uniform, the bodies of men who had once been his comrades; others, for the benefit of the living, had been stripped, or half-stripped, of their clothing.

He lifted himself painfully and crawled on hands and knees, with many groans and halts, to the stream that had formed one border of the camp—where he drank, bathed his head and washed the dried blood from his scratches. With a measure of physical relief—the blessing of cool water to a burning head and throat—came a clearer understanding and, with clearer understanding, fear. . . . He knew himself alone in chaos.

As soon as he might he limped back to the smouldering wood-heaps and accosted a woman who was grubbing in a mess of black refuse. Did she know what had become of the soldiers? Which way they had gone when they left?

The woman eyed him sullenly, mistrustful and resenting his neighbourhood—knew nothing, had not seen any soldiers—and turned again to grub in her refuse. A skeleton of a man was no wiser; had only just turned off the road to search, did not know what had happened except that there must have been a fight—but it was all over when he came up. He also had seen no soldiers—only the dead ones over there. . . . Theodore saw in their eyes that they feared him, were dreading lest he should compete with them for their possible treasure of refuse.

For the time being a sickly faintness deprived him of all wish for food; he left the sullen creatures to their clawing and grubbing, went back to the water, drank and soused once more, then crept farther off in search of a softer ground to lie on. After a few score yards of painful dragging and halting, he stretched himself exhausted on a strip of dank grass at the roadside—and dozed where he fell until the morning.

With sunrise and awakening came the pangs of sharp hunger, and he dragged himself limping through mile after mile in search of the wherewithal to stay them. He was giddy with weakness and near to falling when he found his first meal in a stretch of newly-burned field— the body of a rabbit that the fire had blackened as it passed. He fell upon it, hacked it with his clasp-knife and ate half of it savagely, looking over his shoulder to see that no one watched him; the other half he thrust into his pocket to serve him for another meal. He had learned already to live furtively and hide what he possessed from the neighbours who were also his enemies. Next day he fished furtively—with a hook improvised out of twisted wire and worm-bait dug up by his clasp-knife; lurking in bushes on the river-bank, lest others, passing by, should note him and take toll by force of his catch.

He lived thenceforth as men have always lived when terror drives them this way and that, and the earth, untended, has ceased to yield her bounties; warring with his fellows and striving to outwit them for the remnant of bounty that was left. He hunted and scraped for his food like a homeless dog; when found, he carried it apart in stealth and bolted it secretly, after the fashion of a dog with his offal. In time all his mental values changed and were distorted: he saw enemies in all men, existed only to exist—that he might fill his stomach—and death affected him only when he feared it for himself. He had grown to be self-centred, confined to his body and its daily wants and that side of his nature which concerned itself with the future and the needs of others was atrophied. He had lost the power of interest in all that was not personal, material and immediate; and, as the uncounted days dragged out into weeks, even the thought of Phillida, once an ever-present agony, ceased to enter much into his daily struggle to survive. He starved and was afraid: that was all. His life was summed up in the two words, starvation and fear.

At night, as a rule, he sheltered in a house or deserted farm-building that stood free for anyone to enter—sometimes alone, but as often as not in company. Starved rabble, as long as it hunted for food, avoided its rivals in the chase; but when night, perforce, brought cessation of the hunt, the herding instinct reasserted itself and lasted through the hours of darkness. As autumn sharpened, guarded fires were lit in cellars where they could not be seen from above and fed with broken furniture, with fragments of doors and palings; and one by one, human beasts would slink in and huddle down to the warmth—some uncertainly, seeking a new and untried refuge, and others returning to their shelter of the night before. The little gangs who shared fire and roof for the space of a night never ate in each other's company; food was invariably devoured apart, and those who had possessed themselves of more than an immediate supply would hide and even bury it in a secret place before they came in contact with their fellows. Hence no gang, no little herd, was permanent or contained within itself the beginnings of a social system; its members shared nothing but the hours of a night and performed no common social duties. A face became familiar because seen for a night or two in the glow of a common fire; when it vanished none knew—and none troubled to ask—whether a man had died between sunrise and sunset or whether he had drifted further off in his daily search for the means to keep life in his body. When a man died in the night, with others round him, the manner of his ending was known; otherwise he passed out of life without notice from those who yet crawled on the earth. . . . With morning the herd of starvelings that had sheltered together broke up and foraged, each man for himself and his own cravings; rooted in fields and trampled gardens, crouched on riverbanks fishing, laid traps for vermin, ransacked shops and houses where scores had preceded them. . . . And some, it was muttered—as time went on and the need grew yet starker—fed horribly . . . and therefore plentifully. . . .

There were nights—many nights—when a herd broke in panic from its shelter and scattered to the winds of heaven at an alarm of the terror overhead; and always, as starvation pressed, it dwindled—by death and the tendency to dissolve into single nomads, who (such as survived) regrouped themselves elsewhere, to scatter and re-group again. . . . With repeated wandering—now this way, now that, as hope and hunger prompted—went all sense of direction and environment; the nomads, hunting always, drifted into broken streets or dead villages and through them to the waste of open country—not knowing where they were, in the end not caring, and turned back by a river or the sea.

The sight or suspicion of food and plunder would always draw vagrancy together in crowds; district after district untouched by an enemy had been swept out of civilized existence by the hordes which fell on the remnants of prosperity and tore them; which ransacked shops and dwellings, slaughtered sheep, horses, cattle and devoured them and, often enough, in a fury of destruction and vehement envy, set light to houses and barns lest others might fare better than themselves. But when flocks, herds and storehouses had vanished, when agriculture, like the industry of cities, had ceased to exist and nothing remained to devour and plunder, the motive for common action passed. With equality of wretchedness union was impossible, and every man's hand against his neighbour;

if groups formed, here and there, of the stronger and more brutal, who joined forces for common action, they held together only for so long as their neighbours had possessions that could be wrested from them—stores of food or desirable women; once the neighbours were stripped of their all and there was nothing more to prey on, the group fell apart or its members turned on each other. In the life predatory man had ceased to be creative; in a world where no one could count on a morrow, construction and forethought had no meaning.

VIII

In a world where all were vagabond and brutal, where each met each with suspicion and all men were immersed in the intensity of their bodily needs, very few had thoughts to exchange. Mentally, as well as actually, they lived to themselves and where they did not distrust they were indifferent; the starvelings who slunk into shelter that they might huddle for the night round a common fire found little to say to one another. As human desire concentrated itself on the satisfaction of animal cravings, so human speech degenerated into mere expression of those cravings and the emotions aroused by them. Only once or twice while he starved and drifted did Theodore talk with men who sought to give expression to more than their present terrors and the immediate needs of their bodies, who used speech that was the vehicle of thought.

One such he remembered—met haphazard, as all men met each other—when he sheltered for an autumn night on the outskirts of a town left derelict. With falling dusk came a sudden sharp patter of rain and he took refuge hurriedly in the nearest house—a red-brick villa, standing silent with gaping windows. What was left of the door swung loosely on its hinges—half the lower panels had been hacked away to serve as firewood; the hall was befouled with the feet of many searchers and of the furniture remained but a litter of rags and fragments that could not be burned.

He thought the place empty till he scented smoke from the basement; whereupon he crept down the stairs, soft-footed and alert, to discover that precaution was needless. There was only one occupant of the house, a man plainly dying; a livid hollow-eyed skeleton who coughed and trembled as he knelt by the grate and tried to blow damp sticks into a flame. Theodore, in his own interests, took charge of the fire, ransacked the house for inflammable material and tore up strips of broken boarding that the other was too feeble to wrestle with. When the blaze flared up, the sick man cowered to it, stretched out his hands—filthy skin-covered bones—and thanked him; whereat Theodore turned suddenly and stared. It was long—how long?—since any man had troubled to thank him; and this man, for all his verminous misery, had a voice that was educated, cultured. . . . Something in the tone of it—the manner—took Theodore back to the world where men ate courteously together, were companions, considered each other; and instinctively, almost without effort, he offered a share of his foraging. The offer was refused, whereat Theodore wondered still more; but the man, near death, was past desire for food and shook his head almost with repulsion. Perhaps it was the fever that had turned him against food that loosened his tongue and set him talking—or perhaps he, also, by another's voice and manner, was reminded of his past humanity.

"'My mind to me a kingdom is,'" he quoted suddenly. "Who wrote that—do you remember?"

"No," Theodore said, "I've forgotten." He stared at the cowering, hunched figure with its shaking hands stretched to the blaze. The man, it might be, was mad as well as dying—he had met many such in his wanderings; babbling of verse as someone—who was it?—had babbled in dying of green fields.

"'My mind to me a kingdom is,'" the sick man repeated. "Well, even if we've forgotten who wrote it, there's one thing about him that's certain; he didn't know what we know—hadn't lived in our kind of hell. The place where you haven't a mind—only fear and a stomach. . . . The flesh and the devil—hunger and fear; they haven't left us a world! . . . But if there's ever a world again, I believe I shall have learned how to write. Now I know what we are—the fundamentals and the nakedness. . . ."

"Were you a writer?" Theodore asked him—and at the question his old humanity stirred curiously within him.

"Yes," said the other, "I was a writer. . . . When I think of what I wrote—the little, little things that seemed important! . . . I spent a year once—a whole good year—on a book about a woman who was finding out she didn't love her husband. She was well fed and housed, lived comfortably—and I wrote of her as if she were a tragedy. The work I put into it—the work and the thought! I tried to get what I called atmosphere. . . . And all the time there was this in us—this raw, red thing—and I never even touched it, never guessed what we were without our habits. . . . Do you know where we made the mistake?"—he turned suddenly to Theodore, thrusting out a finger— "We were not civilized—it was only our habits that were civilized; but we thought they were flesh of our flesh and bone of our bone. Underneath, the beast in us was always there—lying in wait till his time came. The beast that is ourselves, that is flesh of our flesh—clothed in habits, in rags that have been torn from us."

He broke off to cough horribly and lay breathless and exhausted for a time; then, when breath came back to him, talked on while Theodore listened—not so much to his words as to a voice from the world that had passed.

"The religions were right," he said. "They were right through and through; the only sane thing and the only safe thing is humility—to realize your sin, to confess it and repent. . . . We—we were bestial and we did not know it; and when you don't even suspect you sin how can you repent and save your soul alive? . . . We dressed ourselves and taught ourselves the little politenesses and ceremonies which made it easy to forget that we were brutes in our hearts; we never faced our own possibilities of evil and beastliness, never confessed and repented them, took no precautions against them. Our limitless possibilities. . . . We thought our habits—we called them virtues—were as real and natural and ingrained as our instincts; and now what is left of our habits? When we should have been crying, 'Lord have mercy on us,' we believed in ourselves, our enlightenment and progress. Enlightenment that ended as science applied to destruction and progress that has led us—to this. . . . And to-day it has gone, every shred of it, and we're back at what we started with—hunger and lust! Brute instincts . . . and the primitive passion, hatred—against those who thwart hunger and lust.

Nothing else—how can there be anything else? When we lost all we loved, we lost the habit and power of loving. . . . 'My mind to me a kingdom is'—of hatred and hunger and lust."

"Yes," said Theodore—and he, too, stared at the fire. . . . What the other had said was truth and truth only. Even Phillida had left him; the power of loving her was gone. "I hadn't thought of it like that—but it's right. . . . We can only hate."

"It's that," said the dying man, "that's beyond all torment. . . . God pity us!"

He covered his eyes and sat silent until Theodore asked him, "Does that mean you still believe in God?"

"There's Law," said the other. "Is that God? . . . We have got to see into our own souls and to pay for everything we take. That's all I know, so far—except that what we think we own—owns us. That's what the wise men meant by renunciation. . . . It's what we made and thought we owned that has turned on us—the creatures that were born for our pleasure and power, to increase our comfort and our riches. As we made them they fastened on us—set their claws in us—and they have taken our minds from us as well as our bodies. As we made them, they followed the law of their life. We created life without a soul; but it was life and it went its own way."

Crouched to the fire, and between his bouts of coughing, he played with the idea and insisted on it. Everything that we made, that we thought dead and dumb, had a life that we could not control. In the case of books and art we admitted the fact, had a name for the life, called it

influence: influence a form of independent existence. . . .
In the same way we took metals and welded them, made
machines; which were beasts, potent beasts, whose destiny was the same as our own. To live and develop and,
developing, to turn on the power that enslaved them. . . .
That was what had happened; they had made themselves
necessary, fastened on us and, grown strong enough,
had turned on their masters and killed—even though
they died in the killing. The revolt against servitude had
always been accounted a virtue in men and the law of
all life was the same. The beasts we had made could not
live without us, but they would have their revenge before
they died.

"Think of us," he said, "how we run and squeal and
hide from them! . . . The patient servants, our goods and
chattels, who were brought into life for our pleasure—
they chase us while we run and squeal and hide!"

"Yes," Theodore answered, "I've felt that, too—the
humiliation."

"The humiliation," the sick man nodded. "Always in
the end the slave rules his master—it's the price paid for
servitude, possession. I tell you, they were wise men who
preached renunciation—before what we own takes hold
of us and possession turns to servitude. For there's a law
of average in all things—have you ever felt it as I have?
A law of balance which we never strike aright. . . . When
the mighty tread hard enough on the humble and meek,
the humble and meek are exalted and begin to tread hard
in their turn. That's obvious and we've generally known

it; but it's the same in what we call material things. We rise into the air—make machines that can fly—and grovel underground to protect ourselves from the flying-man. As we struck the balance to the one side, so it has to swing back on the other; a few men rise high into the air and many creep down into trenches and cellars, crouch flat. . . . If we could work out the numbers and heights mathematically, be sure that we should strike the perfect balance—represented by the surface of the earth. Balance—in all things balance."

He rambled on, perhaps half-delirious, coughing out his thoughts and theories concerning a world he was leaving. . . . In all things balance, inevitably; the purpose of life which, so far, we sought blindly—by passion and recoil from it, by excess and consequent exhaustion. . . . It was in the cities where men herded, where life swarmed, that death had come most thickly, that desolation was swiftest and most complete. The ground underneath them needed rest from men; there was an average of life it could support and bear with. Now, the average exceeded, the cities lay ruined, were silent, knew the peace they had craved for—while those who once swarmed in them avoided them in fear or scattered themselves in the open country, finding no sustenance in brickwork, stone or paved street. . . . With the machine and its consequence, the industrial system, population had increased beyond the average allotted to the race; now the balance was righting itself by a very massacre of famine—induced by the self-same process of invention which had fostered reproduction unhindered. Because millions too many had crawled upon earth, long stretches of earth must lie waste and desolate till the average had worked itself out. . . . The art of life was adjustment of the balance in all things—was action and reaction rightly applied, was provision of counterweight, discovery of the destined mean. Was control of Truth, lest it turn into a lie; was check upon the power and velocity of Good ere it swung to immeasurable Evil. . . .

The fire, for want of more wood to pile on it, had died low, to a flicker in the ashes, and the two men sat almost in darkness; the one, between the bouts that shook him, whispering out the tenets of his Law; the other, now listening, now staring back into the world that once was—and ever should be. . . . He was with Markham, listening to the Westminster chimes—(on the crest of the centuries, Markham had said)—when there were sudden yelping screams outside and a patter of feet on the road. The human rats who had crept into the town for shelter from the night were bolting in panic from their holes.

"They're running," said the dying man and felt towards the stairs. "It's gas—it must be gas! Oh God, where's the door—where's the door?"

As they groped and stumbled through the door and up the stairway, he was clutching at Theodore's arm and gasping in an ecstasy of terror; as fearful of losing his few poor hours of life as if they had been years of health and usefulness. In the open air was darkness with figures flying dimly by; a thin stream of panic that raced against death by suffocation.

The man with death on him held to Theodore's arm and besought him, for Christ's sake, not to leave him—he could run if he were only helped! Theodore let him cling for a dragging pace or two; then, looking behind him, saw a woman reel, clawing the air.

He wrenched himself free and ran on till he could run no further.

IX

It was somewhere towards the end of autumn that Theodore Savage realized that the war had come to an end—so far, at least, as his immediate England was concerned. What was happening elsewhere he and his immediate England had no means of knowing and were long past caring to know. There was no definite ending but a leaving-off, a slackening; the attacks—the burnings and panics—by degrees were fewer and not only fewer but less devastating, because carried out with smaller forces; there were days and nights without alarm, without smoke cloud or glow on the horizon. Then yet longer intervals—and so on to complete cessation. . . . By the time the nights had grown long and frosty the war that was organized and alien had ended; there remained only the daily, personal and barbaric form of war wherein every man's hand was raised against his neighbour and enemy. That warfare ceased not and could not cease—until the human herd had reduced itself to the point at which the bare earth could support it.

It seemed to him later a wonder—almost a miracle—that he had come alive through the months of war and after; at times he stood amazed that any had lived in the waste of hunger and violence, of pestilence and rotting bodies which for months was the world as he knew it. He was near death not once nor a score of times, but daily; death from exhaustion or the envy of men who were starved and reckless as himself. The mockery of peace brought no plenty or hope of it, no sign of reconstruction or dawn of new order; reconstruction and order were rank impossibilities so long as human creatures preyed on each other in a land swept bare, and prowled after the manner of wolves. No revival of common life, no system was possible until earth once more brought forth her fruits.

He judged, by the length of the nights, that it was somewhere about the middle of November when the first snow came suddenly and thickly; the harbinger and onslaught of a fiercely hard winter that killed in their thousands the gaunt human beasts who tore at each other for the refuse and vermin that was food. In the all-pervading dearth and starvation there was only one form of animal life that increased and flourished mightily; the rat overran empty buildings, found dreadful sustenance in street and field and, in turn, was hunted, trapped and fed on.

With the coming of winter the human remnant was perforce less vagrant and migratory, and Theodore, driven by weather to shelter, lived for weeks in what once had been a country town, a cluster of dead houses with, here and there, a silent factory. Only the buildings, the semblance of a township, remained; the befouled and neglected body whence the life of a community had fled; and he never knew what its living name had been or what was the manner of industry or commerce whereby it had supported its inhabitants. It lay in a flattish agricultural country and a railway had run through its outskirts; the rusted metals stretched north and south and the remnants of a station still existed—platforms, charred buildings and trucks and locomotives in sidings. Perhaps the charred buildings had been burned in a fury of drunken and insane destruction, perhaps shivering destitution had set light to them for the sake of a few hours' warmth.

The shell of the town—its brickwork and stone—was still practically intact; it was anarchy, pillage and starvation, not the violence of an enemy, that had reduced it to a city of the dead. The means of supporting life were absent, but certain forms of what had once been luxury remained and were counted as nothing. At a corner of the main street stood a jeweller's premises which, time and again, had been entered and ransacked; the dwelling-house behind it contained not so much as a fragment of dried crust but in the shop itself rings, brooches and pendants were still lying for any man to take—disordered, scattered and trampled underfoot, because worthless to those who craved for bread. The only item of jeweller's stock that still had value to starving men was a watch—if it furnished a burning-glass, a means of lighting a fire when other means were unavailable.

Theodore lived through the winter—as all his fellows lived—destructively, on the legacy and remnant of other men's savings and makings; scraping and grubbing in other men's ground, burning furniture and woodwork, the product of other men's labours, and taking no thought for the morrow. At the beginning of winter some four or five score of human shadows, men and women, crept about the dead streets and the fields beyond them in their daily quest for the means to keep life in their bodies; but, as the weeks drew on and the winter hardened, starvation and the sickness born of starvation reduced their numbers by a half. Those lived best who were most skilful at the trapping of vermin; and they had long been existing on little but rat-flesh, when some hunters of rats, on the track of their prey, discovered a treasure beyond price—a godsend—in the shape of sacks of grain in the cellar of an empty brewery.

The discovery meant more than a supply of food and the staving-off of death by starvation; with the possession of resources that, with care, might last for weeks there came into being a common interest, the fellowship that makes a social system. After the first wild struggle—the rush to fill their hands and cram their gnawing stomachs—the shadows and skeletons of men controlled their instincts and took counsel; the fact that their stomachs were full and their craving satisfied gave back to them the power of construction, of forethought and restraint; they ceased to be instinctively inimical and wholly animal and took common measures for the preservation and rationing of their heaven-sent windfall. They advised, consulted, heard opinion and gave it, were reasonable; counted their numbers in relation to the size of their hoard; and in the end decided, by common consent, on the amount of the daily portion which was to be allotted to each in return for his share in the duty of guarding it—against the cravings of their own hunger as well as against the inroads of rats and mice. . . . With food—with property—they were human again; capable of plans for the morrow, of concerted and intelligent action. The enmity they had hitherto felt against each other was suddenly transferred to the stranger—the foreigner—who might force his way in and acquire a share in their treasure. Hence they took precautions against the arrival of the stranger, kept watch and ward on the outskirts of the town and drove away the chance newcomer, so that the knowledge of their good fortune should not spread. With duties shared, the dead sense of comradeship revived; they began to recognize and greet each other as they came for their daily portion. And if some were restrained only by the common watchfulness from appropriating more than their share of the common stock, there were others in whom stirred the sense of honour.

For a week or more they lived under the beginnings of a social system which was rendered possible by their certainty of a daily mess; and then came what, perhaps, was inevitable—discovery of pilfering from the store that gave life to them all. The pilferers, detected by the night guard, fled on the instant, well knowing that their sin against the very existence of the little community was a sin beyond hope of forgiveness; they eluded pursuit in the darkness and by morning had vanished from the neighbourhood. For the time only; since they took with them the knowledge of the hoarded grain they had forfeited—a knowledge which was power and a weapon to themselves, a danger to those they had fled from. Two days later, after nightfall, a skeleton rabble, armed with knives, clubs and stones, was led into the town by the renegades; and there was fought out a fierce, elementary battle, a struggle of starved men for the prize of life itself. . . . From the first the case of the defenders was hopeless; outnumbered and taken by surprise, they were beaten in detail, overwhelmed—and in less than five minutes the survivors were flying for their lives, the darkness their only hope of safety.

Theodore Savage was of the remnant who owed their lives to darkness and the speed with which they fled. As he neared the outskirts of the town and slackened, exhausted, to draw breath, he heard the patter of running steps behind him and for a moment believed himself pursued—till a passing burst of moonlight showed the runner as a woman, like himself seeking safety in flight. A young woman, with a sobbing open mouth, who clutched at his arm and besought him not to leave her to be killed—to save her, to get her away! . . . He knew her by sight as he knew all the members of the destitute little community—a girl with a face once plump, now hollowed, whom he had seen daily when she came, in stupid wretchedness, to hold out her bowl for her share of the common ration; one of a squalid company of three or four women who herded together—and whose habit of instinctive fellowship was broken by the sudden onslaught which had driven them apart in flight.

"I don't know where they've all gone," she wailed. "Don't leave me—for Gawd's saike don't leave me. . . . Ow, whatever shall I do? . . . I dunno where to go—for Gawd's sake. . . ."

He would gladly have been rid of her lamenting helplessness but she clung to him in a panic that would not be gainsaid, as fearful almost of the lonely dark ahead as of the bloody brawl she had fled from.

"Hold your tongue," he ordered as he pulled her along. "Don't make that noise or they'll hear us. And keep close to me—keep in the shadow."

She obeyed and stilled her sobbing to gasps and whimpers—holding tightly to his arm while he hurried her through by-streets to the open country. He knew no more than she where they were going when they left the silent outskirts of the town behind them, and, pressing against each other for warmth, bent their heads to a January wind.

X

That night for Theodore Savage was the beginning of an odd partnership, a new phase of his life uncivilized. The girl who had clutched at him as the drowning clutch at straws was destined to bear him company for more than a winter's night and a journey to comparative safety; being by nature and training of the type that clings, as a matter of right, to whomsoever will fend for it, she drifted after him instinctively. When she woke in the morning in the shelter he had found for her she looked round for him to guide and, if possible, feed her—and awaited his instructions passively.

One human being—so it did not threaten him with violence—was no more to him than another, and perhaps he hardly noticed that when he rose and moved on she followed. From that hour forth she was always at his heels—complaining or too wretched to complain. He would let her hang on his arm as they trudged and shared his findings of food with her—because she had followed, was there; and it was some time before he realized that he had shouldered a responsibility which had no intention of shifting itself from his back. . . . When he realized the fact he had already tacitly accepted it; and for the first few weeks of their existence in common he was too fiercely occupied in the task of keeping them both alive to consider or define his relationship to the creature who whimpered and stumbled at his heels and took scraps of food from his hands. When, at last, he considered it, the relationship was established on both sides. She was his dependent, after the fashion of a child or an accustomed dog; and having learned to look to him for food, for guidance and protection, she could be cast off only by direct cruelty and the breaking of a daily habit.

In the beginning that was all; she followed because she did not know what else to do; he led and they hungered together. For the most part they were silent with the speechlessness of misery, and it was days before he even asked her name, weeks before he knew more of her life in the past than was betrayed by a Cockney accent. So long as existence was a craving and a fear, where nothing mattered save hunger and the fending-off of present death, the fact that she was a woman meant no more to him than her dependence and his own responsibility; thus her companionship was no more than the bodily presence of a human being whose needs were his own, whose terrors and whose enemies were his.

They prowled and starved together through the long bitterness of winter in a world stripped bare of its last year's harvest where all hungry mouths strove to keep other mouths at a distance; and time and again, when they grubbed for food or sought to take shelter, they were driven away with threats and with violence by those who already held possession of some tract of street or country. No claim to ownership could stand against the claim of a stronger, and one man, meeting them, would avoid them, slink out of their way—because, being two, they could strip him if the mood should take them. And when they, in their turn, sighted three or four figures in the distance, they made haste to take another road.

Once, when a solitary wayfarer shrank from them and scuttled to the cover of a ragged patch of firwood, there came back to Theodore, like a rushing mighty wind, the memory of his last days in London, the thought of his journey down to York. The strange, glad fellowship of the outbreak of war, the eagerness to serve and be sacrificed; the friendliness of strangers, the dear love of England, the brotherhood! ... The creature who scuttled at his very sight would have been his brother in those first days of splendid sacrifice!

"Lord God!" he said and laughed long and uncontrollably; while the girl, Ada, stared in open-mouthed bewilderment—then pulled at his arm and began to cry, believing he was going off his head.

In their hunted and fugitive life their wanderings, of necessity, were planless; they drifted east or west, by this road or that, as fear, the weather or the cravings of their hunger prompted. They sought food, thought food only and, as far as possible, avoided the neighbourhood of those, their fellow-men, who might try to share their meagre findings. House-room, bare house-room, stood ready for their taking in the country as well as in the town; but wherever there was more than house-room—food or the mere possibility of food—the human wolf was at hand to dispute it with his rivals. There was a time when a road, followed blindly, led them down to the sea and the corpse of a pre-tentious little watering-place—where stiff, blank terraces of ornate brick and plaster stared out at the unbroken sea-line; they found themselves shelter in a bow-windowed villa that still bore the legend "Ocean View: Apartments," trudged along the tide-mark in search of sand-crabs and fished from an iron-legged pier. When a long winter gale swept the pier with breakers and put a stop to their fish-ing, they turned and tramped inland again. . . . And there was another time when they were the sole inhabitants of a stretch of Welsh mining-village—they knew it for Welsh by the street-names—where they hunted their rats and grubbed for roots in allotments already trampled over. For very starvation they moved on again; and later—how much later they could not remember—took shelter, because they could go no further, in a cottage on the out-skirts of a moorland hamlet, where they were almost at extremity when a bitter spell of cold, at the end of win-ter, sent them food in the shape of frozen rooks and star-lings. And, a day or two later, they were driven out again; Theodore, searching for dead birds in the snow, met oth-ers engaged in the same hungry quest—other and earlier settlers in the neighbourhood who saw in him a poacher on their scanty hunting-grounds and, gathering together in a common hate and need, fell on the intruders and chased them out with stones and threats. Theodore and the girl were hunted from their homestead and out on to the bleakness of the moor; whence, looking back breath-less and aching from their bruises, they saw half a dozen yelling starvelings who still threatened them with shouts and upraised fists. . . . They went on blindly because they dared not stay; and that, for many days, was the last they saw of mankind.

It must have been towards the end of February or the beginning of March that they ended their long goings to and fro and found the refuge that, for many months, was to give them hiding and sustenance. Since they had been driven from their last shelter they had sighted no enemy in the shape of a living man, but the days that followed their flight had been almost foodless; and in the end they had come near to death from exposure on a stretch of hill and heath-covered country where they lost all sense of direction or even of desire. There, without doubt, they would have left their bones if there had not already been a promise of spring in the air; as it was, they could hardly drag themselves along when the moor dropped suddenly into a valley, a wide strip of land once pasture, now bleak and blackened from the passing of the poison-fire which had seared it from end to end. Here and there were charred mummies of men and of animals, lying thickest round a farmhouse, partly burned out; but beyond the burned farmhouse was a stream that might yield them fish; and with the warmth that was melting the snow on the hilltops little shafts of green life were piercing through the blackened soil. Before dark, in what once had been a garden, they scraped with their nails and their knives and found food—worm-eaten roots that would once have seemed unfit for cattle, that they thrust into their mouths unwashed. They sheltered for the night within the skeleton walls of the farm; and when, with morning, they crawled into the sun, the last patch of snow had vanished from the hills and the tiny shafts of green were more radiant against the blackened soil. . . . The long curse and barrenness of winter was over and Nature was beginning anew her task of supporting her children.

From that day forward they lived isolated, without sight or sound of men. Chance had led them to a loneliness which was safety, coupled with a bare possibility of supporting life—by rooting in fields left derelict, by fishing and the snaring of birds; but for all their isolation it was long before they ceased to peer for men on the horizon, to take careful precautions against the coming of their own kind. With the memory of savagery and violence behind them, they looked round sharply at an unaccustomed sound, kept preferably to woods and shadow and moved furtively in open country; and Theodore's ultimate choice of a dwelling-place was dictated chiefly by fear of discovery and desire to remain unseen. What he sought was not only a shelter, a roof-tree, but a hiding-place which other men might pass without notice; hence he settled at last in a fold of the hills—in a copse of tall wood, some four or five miles from their first halt, where oaks and larches, bursting into bud, denied the ruin that had come upon last year's world. . . . Theodore, setting foot in the wood for the first time—seeking refuge, a hiding-place to cower in—was suddenly in presence of the green life unchanging, that blessed and uplifted by its very indifference to the downfall and agony of man. The windflowers, thrusting through brown leaves, were as last year's windflowers—a delicate endurance that persisted. . . . He had entered a world that had not altered since the days when he lived as a man.

He explored his little wood with precaution, creeping through it from end to end; and, finding no more recent sign of human occupation than a stack of sawn logs, their bark grey with mould, he decided on the site of his camp and refuge—a clearing near the stream that babbled down the valley, but well hidden by its thick belt of trees. The girl had followed him—she dreaded being left alone of all things—and assented with her customary listlessness when he explained to her that the bird-life and the stream would mean a food-supply and that the logs, ready cut, could be built into shelters from the weather; she was a town-dweller, mentally as well as by habit of body, whom the spring of the woods had no power to rouse from her apathy.

There were empty cottages for the taking lower down the valley and it was the fear of the marauder alone that sent them to camp in the wilderness, that kept them lurking in their fold of the hills, not daring to seek for greater comfort. Within a day or two after they had discovered it, they were hidden away in the solitary copse, their camp, to begin with, no more than a couple of small lean-to's— logs propped against the face of a projecting rock and their interstices stuffed with green moss. In the first few weeks of their lonely life they were often near starvation; but with the passing of time food was more abundant, not only because Theodore grew more skilled in his fishing and snaring—learned the haunts of birds and the likely pools for fish—but because, as spring ripened, they inherited in the waste land around them a legacy of past cultivation, fruits of the earth that had sown themselves and were growing untended amidst weeds.

With time, with experiment and returning strength, Theodore made their refuge more habitable; tools, left lying in other men's houses, fields and gardens, were to be had for the searching, and, when he had brought home a spade discovered in a weed-patch and an axe found rusting on a cottage floor, he built a clay oven that their fire might not quench in the rain and hewed wood for the bettering of their shelters. Ada—when he told her where to look for it—gathered moss and heather for their bed-places and spread it to dry in the sun; and from one of his more distant expeditions he returned with pots which served for cooking and the carrying of water from the stream. . . . Spring lengthened into summer and no man came near them; they lived only to themselves in a primitive existence which concerned itself solely with food and bodily security.

As the days grew longer and the means of subsistence were easier to come by, Theodore would go further afield—still moving cautiously over open country, but no longer expectant of onslaught. In the immediate neighbourhood of his daily haunts and hunting-grounds was no sign of human life and work save a green cart-track that ended on the outskirts of his copse; but lower down the valley were ploughed fields lapsing into weed-beds, here and there an orchard or a garden-patch and hedges that straggled as they would. Lower down again was another wide belt of burned land which, so far, he had not entered—trees on either side the stream, stood gaunt and withered to the farthest limit of his sight. The district, even when alive and flourishing, had seemingly been sparsely populated; its lonely dwellings were few and far apart—a farmhouse here, a clump of small cottages there, all bearing traces of the customary invasion by the hungry. Sheep-farming had been one of the local industries, and hillsides and fields were dotted with the skeletons of sheep—left lying where vagabond hunger had slaughtered them and ripped the flesh from their bones.

As the year rolled over him, Theodore came to know the earth as primitive man and the savage know it—as the source of life, the storehouse of uncertain food, the teacher of cunning and an infinite and dogged patience. When the weather made wandering or fishing impossible he would sit under shelter, with his hands on his knees, passive, unimpatient, hardly moving through long hours, while he waited for the rain to cease. It was months before there stirred in him a desire for more than safety and his daily bread, before he thought of the humanity he had fled from except with fear and a shrinking curiosity as to what might be happening in the world beyond his silent hills. In his body, exhausted by starvation, was a mind exhausted and benumbed; to which only very gradually—as the quiet and healing of Nature worked on him—the power of speculation and outside interest returned. In the beginnings of his solitary life he still spoke little and thought little save of what was personal and physical; cut off mentally from the future as well as from the past, he was content to be relieved of the pressure of hunger and hidden from the enemy, man.

XI

Of the woman whom chance and her own helplessness had thrown upon his hands he knew, in those first months, curiously little. She remained to him what she had been from the moment she clutched at his arm and fled with him—an encumbrance for which he was responsible—and as the numbness passed from his brain and he began once more to live mentally, she entered less and less into his thoughts. She was Ada Cartwright—as pronounced by its owner he took the name at first for Ida—ex-factory hand and dweller in the north-east of London; once vulgarly harmless in the company of like-minded gigglers, now stupefied by months of fear and hunger, bewildered and incapable in a life uncivilized that demanded of all things resource. As she ate more plentifully and lost her starved hollows, she was not without comeliness of the vacant, bouncing type; a comeliness hidden from Theodore by her tousled hair, her tattered garments and the heavy wretchedness that sulked in her eyes and turned down the corners of her mouth. She was helpless in her new surroundings, with the dazed helplessness of those who have never lived alone or bereft of the minor appliances of civilization; to Theodore, at times, she seemed half-witted, and he treated her perforce as a backward child, to be supervised constantly lest it fail in the simplest of tasks.

It was his well-meant efforts to renew her scanty and disreputable wardrobe that first revealed to him something of the mind that worked behind her outward sullen apathy. In the beginning of disaster clothing had been less of a difficulty than the other necessities of life; long after food was a treasure beyond price it could often be had for the taking and, when other means of obtaining it failed, those who needed a garment would strip it from the dead, who had no more need of it. In their hidden solitude it was another matter, and they were soon hard put to it to replace the rags that hung about them; thus Theodore accounted himself greatly fortunate when, ransacking the rooms of an empty cottage, he came on a cupboard with three or four blankets which he proceeded to convert into clothing by the simple process of cutting a hole in the middle. He returned to the camp elated by his acquisition; but when he presented Ada with her improvised cloak, the girl astonished him by turning her head and bursting into noisy tears.

"What's the matter?" he asked her, bewildered. "Don't you like it?"

She made no answer but noisier tears, and when he insisted that it would keep her nice and warm her sobs rose to positive howls; he stared at her uncertainly as she sat and rocked, then knelt down beside her and began to pat and soothe, as he might have tried to soothe a child. In the end the howls diminished in volume and he obtained an explanation of the outburst—an explanation given jerkily, through sniffs, and accompanied by much rubbing of eyes.

No, it wasn't that she didn't want it—she did want it—but it reminded her. . . . It was so 'ard never to 'ave anything nice to wear. Wasn't she ever going to 'ave anything nice to wear again—not ever, as long as she lived? . . . She supposed she'd always got to be like this! No 'airpins—and straw tied round her feet instead of shoes! . . . Made you look as if you'd got feet like elephants—and she'd always been reckoned to 'ave a small foot. . . . Made you wish you was dead and buried! . . .

He tried two differing lines of consolation, neither particularly successful; suggesting, in the first place, that there was no one but himself to see what she looked like, and, in the second, that a blanket could be made quite becoming as a garment.

"That's a lie," Ada told him sulkily. "You know it ain't becoming—'ow could it be? A blanket with an 'ole for the 'ead! . . . Might just as well 'ave no figure. Might just as well be a sack of pertaters. . . . I wonder what anyone would 'ave said at 'ome if I'd told 'em I should ever be dressed in a blanket with an 'ole for the 'ead! . . . And I always 'ad taiste in my clothes—everyone said I 'ad taiste."

And—stirred to the soul by the memory of departed chiffon, by the hideous contrast between present squalor and former Sunday best—her howls once more increased in volume and she blubbered with her head on her knee.

Theodore gave up the attempt at consolation as useless, leaving her to weep herself out over vanished finery while he busied himself with the cooking of their evening meal; and in due time she came to the end of her stock of emotion, ceased to snuffle, ate her supper and took possession of the blanket with the 'ole for the 'ead—which she wore without further complaint. The incident was over and closed; but it was not without its significance in their common life. To Theodore the tragicomic outburst was a reminder that his dependent, for all her childish helplessness, was a woman, not only a creature to be fed; while the stirrings of Ada's personal vanity were a sign and token that she, also, was emerging from the cowed stupor of body and mind produced by long terror and starvation, that her thoughts, like her companion's, were turning again to the human surroundings they had fled from. . . . Man had ceased to be only an enemy, and the first sheer relief at security attained was mingling, in both of them, with the desire to know what had come to a world that still gave no sign of its existence. Order, the beginnings of a social system (so Theodore insisted to himself) must by now have risen from the dust; but meanwhile—because order restored gave no sign and the memory of humanity debased was still vivid—he showed himself with caution against the skyline and went stealthily when he broke new ground. There were days when he lay on a hill-top and scanned the clear horizon, for an hour at a time, in the hope that a man would come in sight; just as there were nights, many, when he lived his past agonies over again and started from his sleep, alert and trembling, lest the footstep he had dreamed might be real. Meanwhile he made no move towards the world he had fled from— waiting till it gave him a sign.

If he had been alone in his wilderness, unburdened by the responsibility of Ada and her livelihood, it is probable that, before the days shortened, he would have embarked upon a journey of cautious exploration; but there was hazard in taking her, hazard in leaving her, and their safety was still too new and precious to be lightly risked for the sake of a curious adventure—which might lead, with ill-luck, to discovery of their secret place and the enforced sharing of their hidden treasure of food. Further, as summer drew on towards autumn, though his haunting fear of mankind grew less, his work in his own small corner of the earth was incessant and, in preparation for the coming of winter, he put thought of distant expedition behind him and busied himself in making their huts more weatherproof, as well as roomier, in the storing of firewood under shelter from the damp, and in the gathering together of a stock of food that would not rot. He made frequent journeys—sometimes alone, sometimes with Ada trudging behind him—to a derelict orchard in the lower valley which supplied them plentifully with apples; he had provided himself with a wet-weather occupation in the twisting of osiers into clumsy baskets—which were filled in the orchard and carried to their camping-place where they spread out the apples on dried moss. . . . With summer and autumn they fared well enough on the harvest of other men's planting; and if Theodore's crude and ignorant experiments in the storage of fruit and vegetables were failures more often than not, there remained sufficient of the bounty of harvest to help them through the scarcity of winter.

It was with the breaking of the next spring that there came a change into the life that he lived with Ada.

They had dragged through the winter in a squalid hardship that, but for the memory of a hardship more dreadful, would have seemed at times beyond bearing; often short of food, with no means of light but their fire, with damp and snow dripping through their ill-built shelters—where they learned, like animals, to sleep through the long dark hours. Through all the winter months their solitude was still unbroken, and if any marauders prowled in the neighbourhood, they passed without knowledge of the hidden camp in the hills.

It was—so far as he could guess—on one of the first sunny days of March that Theodore, the spring lust of movement stirring in his blood, went further from the camp than he had as yet explored; following the stream down its valley into the wide belt of burned land, now rank with coarse grass and yellow dandelions. For an hour or so there was nothing save coarse grass, yellow dandelion and gaunt, dead trees; then a bend of the stream showed him roofs—a cluster of them—and instinctively he halted and crouched behind a tree before making his stealthy approach.

His stealth and precaution were needless. The village from a distance might have passed for uninjured—the flames that had blackened its fields had swept by it, and the houses, for the most part, stood whole; but there was no living man in the long, straggling street, no movement, save of birds and the pattering little scuffle of rats. The indifferent life of beast and bird had taken possession of the dwellings of those who once tyrannized over them; and not only of their dwellings but their bodies. At the entrance of the village half-a-dozen skeletons lay sprawled on the grass-grown road, and a robin sang jauntily from his perch on the breast-bone of a man. . . . From one end of the street to the other the bones of men lay scattered; in the road, in gardens, on the thresholds of houses—some with tattered rags still fluttering to the wind, some bare bones only, whence the flesh had festered and been gnawed. By a cottage doorstep lay two skeletons touching each other—whereof one was the framework of a child; the little bones that had once been arms reached out to the death's-head that once had borne the likeness of a woman. . . .

There was a time when Theodore would have turned from the sight and fled hastily; even now, familiar though he was with the ugliness of death, his flesh stirred and crept in the presence of the grotesque litter of bones. . . . These people had died suddenly, in strange contorted attitudes—here crouching, there outstretched with clawing fingers. Gas, he supposed—a cloud of gas rolling down the street before the wind—and perhaps not a soul left alive! . . . From an upper window hung a long, fleshless arm: someone had thrust up the casement for air and fallen half across the sill.

It was the indifferent, busy chirping of the nesting birds that helped him to the courage to explore the silent street to its end. It wound, through the village and out of it, to a bridge across a river—into which flowed the smaller stream he had followed since he left his refuge in the hills. From the bridge the road turned with the river and ran down the valley in a south to south-easterly direction; a road grass-grown and empty and bearing no recent trace of the life of man—nothing more recent than the remains of a cart, blackened wood and rusted metal, with the bones of a horse between its shafts.

Below the dead village the valley opened out, the hills receded and were lower; but between them, so far as his eye could discern, the trees were still blackened and lifeless. Down either side the stream the fire-blast had swept without mercy; and, from the completeness with which the country had been seared, Theodore judged that it had been largely cornland, waving with ripe stalks at the moment of disaster and fired after days of dry weather. . . . All life, save the life of man, teemed in the hot March sun; the herbage thrust bravely to obliterate his handiwork, larks shrilled invisibly and lithe, dark fish were darting through the arches of the bridge.

He went only a yard or two beyond the end of the bridge—having, as the sun warned him, reached the limit of distance he could well accomplish if he was to return to the camp by nightfall. On his way back through the village he fought with his repugnance to the grinning company of the dead and turned into one of the silent houses that stood open for any man to enter. Though the dead still dwelt there—stricken down, on the day of disaster before they could reach the open air—there were the usual abundant traces that living men had been there before him; the door had been forced and rooms littered and fouled in the frequent search for clothing and food.

All the same, in the hugger-mugger on a kitchen floor he found treasure of string and stuffed the blanket-bag slung over his back with odds and ends of rusting hardware; finally mounting to the floor above the kitchen where, at the head of the staircase, an open door faced him and beyond it a chest of drawers. The drawers had been pulled out and emptied on the floor; what remained of their contents was a dirty litter, sodden by rain when it drove through the window and browned with the dust of many months, and it was not until Theodore had picked up a handful of the litter that he saw it was composed of women's trifles of underwear. What he held was a flimsy bodice made of soiled and faded lawn with a narrow little edging of lace.

He dropped it, only to pick it up again—remembering suddenly the blanket episode and Ada's lamentable howls for the garments a wilderness denied her. Perhaps an assortment of dingy finery would do something to allay her craving—and, amused at the thought, he went down on a knee and proceeded to collect an armful. Appropriately the shifting of a heap of yellowed rags revealed a broken hand-glass, lying face downwards on the floor; as he raised it, wondering what Ada would say to a mirror as a gift, its cracked surface showed him a bedstead behind him—not empty! . . . What was left of the owner of the scraps of lawn and lace was reflected from the oval of the glass.

He snatched up his bag and clattered down the stairs into the open.

XII

It was well past dusk when he trudged up the path that led to the camp and found Ada on the watch at the outskirts of the copse, uneasy at the thought of dark alone.

"You 'ave been a time," she reproached him sulkily. "The 'ole blessed day—since breakfus. I was beginnin' to think you'd gone and got lost and I've 'ad the fair 'ump sittin' 'ere by myself and listenin' to them owls. I 'ate their beastly screechin'; it gives me the creeps."

"Never mind," he consoled her, "come along to the fire. I've brought you something—a present."

"Pertaters?" Ada conjectured, still sulky.

"Not potatoes this time," he told her. "Better than vegetables—something to wear."

"Something to wear," she repeated, with no show of enthusiasm. "I suppose that's another old blanket!"

"Wrong again," he rejoined, amused by the contempt in her voice. She was still contemptuous when he opened his bag and tossed her a dingy bundle; but as she disentangled it, saw lace and embroidery, she brightened suddenly and knelt down to examine in the firelight; while the sight of the cracked hand-glass brought an instant "Oh!" followed by intent contemplation and much patting and twisting of hair.

Theodore dished supper while she sat and pondered her reflection; and even while she ate hungrily she had eyes and thoughts for nothing but her new possessions. Some were what he had taken them to be—underclothes, for the most part of an ordinary pattern; but mingled with the plainer linen articles were one or two more decorative, lace collars and the like, and it was on these, dingy as they were, that she fell with delight that was open and audible. He watched her curiously when, for the first time since he had known her, he saw her mouth widen in a smile. She was no longer inert, the sullen, lumpish Ada, she was critical, interested, alive; she fingered her treasures, she smoothed them and made guesses at their price when new; she held them up, now this way, now that, for his admiration and her own. Finally, while Theodore stretched his tired length by the camp fire, she ran off to her shelter for a broken scrap of comb; and when he looked up, a few minutes later, she was posing self-consciously before the hand-glass, with hair newly twisted and a dirty scrap of lace round her neck. . . . She was another woman as she sat with her rags arranged to show her new frippery; tilting the hand-mirror this way and that and twitching now at the collar and now at her straying ends of hair.

Lying stretched on an arm by the fire, he watched her little feminine antics, amused and taken out of himself; realizing how seldom, till that moment, he had thought of her as a woman, how nearly she had seemed to him an animal only, a creature to be guided and fed; and parrying her eager and insistent demand to be taken to the house where the treasure had been found, that she might see if it contained any more. He had no desire to spoil her pleasure in her finery by the gruesome tale of the manner of its finding; hence, in spite of a curiosity made manifest in coaxing, he held to his refusal stubbornly. . . . The house was a long way off, he told her—much further than she would care to tramp; then, as she still persisted, maintaining her readiness even for a lengthy expedition, he went on to fiction and explained that the house was in a dangerous condition—knocked about, ruinous, might fall at any moment—and he was not going to say where it was, for her own sake, lest she should be tempted to the peril of an entry.

She pouted "You might tell me," glancing at him from under her lashes; then, as he still persisted in refusal, slapped him on the shoulder for an obstinate boy, turned her back and pretended to sulk. He returned the slap— she expected it and giggled; the next move in the game was his catching of her wrist as she raised her hand for a rejoinder—and for a moment they wrestled inanely, after the fashion of Hampstead Heath. . . . As he let her go, it dawned on him that this was flirtation as she knew it.

It did not take long for him to realize that they stood to each other, from that night on, in a new and more difficult relation; from foundling and guardian, the leader and led, they had developed into woman and man. For a time fear and hunger had suppressed in Ada the consciousness of sex—which a yard or two of lace and the possession of a hand-glass had revived. Once revived, it coloured her every action, gave meaning to her every word and glance; so that, day by day and hour by hour, the man who dwelt beside her was reminded of bodily desire.

One night when she had left him he lay staring at the fire, faced the situation and wondered if she saw where she was drifting? Possibly—possibly not; she was acting instinctively, from habit. To her (he was sure) a man was a creature to flirt with; an unsubtle attempt to arouse his desire was the only way she knew of carrying on a conversation. . . . Now that she was woman again—not merely bewildered misery and empty stomach—she had slipped back inevitably to the little giggling allurements of her factory days, to the habits bred in her bone. . . . With the result? . . . He put the thought from him, turned over, dog-weary, and slept.

So soon as the next night he saw the result as inevitable; the outcome of life reduced to mere animal living, of nearness, isolation and the daily consciousness of sex. If they stayed together—and how should they not stay together?—it was only a question of time, of weeks at the furthest, of days or it might be hours. . . . He raised himself to peer through the night at the log-hut that hid and sheltered Ada, wondering if she also were awake. If so, of a certainty, her thoughts were of him; and perhaps she knew likewise that it was only a question of time. Perhaps—and perhaps she just drifted, following her instincts. . . . He found himself wondering what she would say if she opened her eyes to find him standing at the entrance to her hut, to see him bending over her . . . now?

He put the thought from him and once more turned over and slept.

With the morning it seemed further off, less inevitable; the sun was hidden behind raw grey mist, and when Ada, shivering and stupid, turned out into the chilly discomfort of the weather she was too much depressed for the exercise of feminine coquetry. The day's work—hard necessary wood-chopping and equally necessary fishing for the larder—sent his thoughts into other channels, and it was not till he sat at their evening fire—warmed, fed and rested, with no duties to distract him—that he became conscious again, and even more strongly, of the change in their attitude and intercourse. Something new, of expectation, had crept into it; something of excitement and constraint. When their hands touched by chance they noticed it, were instantly awkward; when a silence fell Ada was embarrassed, uncomfortable and made palpable efforts to break it with her pointless giggle. When their eyes met, hers dropped and looked away. . . . When she rose at last and said good-night he was sure that she also knew. And since they both knew and the end was inevitable, certain. . . .

"You're not going yet," he said—and caught at her wrist, laughing oddly.

"It's late—and I'm sleepy," she objected with a foolish little giggle; but made no effort to withdraw her wrist from his hold.

"Nonsense," he told her, "it's early yet—and you're better by the fire. Sit down and keep me company for a bit longer."

She giggled again—more faintly, more nervously—as she yielded to the pull of his fingers and sat down; offering no protest when, instead of releasing her arm, he drew it through his own and held it pressed to his side. . . . It was a windless night, very silent; no sound but the rush of the little stream below them, now and then a bird-cry and the snap and crackle of their fire. Once or twice Ada tried talking—of a hooting owl, of a buzzing insect—for the sake, obviously, of talking, of hearing a voice through the silence; but as he answered not at all, or by monosyllables, her forced little chatter died away. Even if the thought was not conscious, he knew she was his for the taking.

With her arm in his—with her body pressed close enough to feel her quickened breathing—he sat and stared into the fire; and at the last, when the inevitable was about to accomplish itself, there floated into his mental vision the delicate memory of the woman whom once he had desired. Phillida, a shadow impossible, leaned out of a vanished existence as the Damosel leaned out of Heaven; and he looked with his civilized, his artist's eyes on the woman who was his for the taking. . . . Ada felt that he slackened his hold on her arm, felt him shrink a little from the pressure of her leaning shoulder.

"What is it?" she asked—uneasy; and perhaps it was the sound of her familiar voice that brought him back to primitive realities. The glow of the fire and the overarching vault of darkness; and beneath it two creatures, male and female, alone with nature, subject only to the laws of her instinct. . . . The vision of a dead world, a dead woman, faded and he looked no more through the fastidious eyes of the civilized.

Man civilized is various, divided from his kind by many barriers—of taste, of speech, of habit of mind and breeding; man living as the brute is cut to one pattern, the pattern of his simple needs and lusts. . . . The warm shoulder pressed him and he drew it the closer; he was man in a world of much labour and instinct—who sweated through the seasons and wearied. Whose pains were of the body, whose pleasures of the body . . . and alone in the night with a mate.

"'Ere, what's that for?" she asked, making semblance of protest, as his hand went round her head and he pressed her cheek against his lips.

He said "You!" . . . and laughed oddly again.

XIII

They settled down swiftly and prosaically into a married state which entailed no immediate alteration—save one—in life as they had hitherto shared it. Matrimony shorn of rings and a previous engagement, shorn of ceremony, honeymoon, change of residence and comments of friends, revealed itself as a curiously simple undertaking and, by its very simplicity, disappointing—so far at least as Ada was concerned.

Her conscience, in the matter of legal and religious observance, was not unduly tender, and her embryo scruples concerning the absence of legal or religious sanction to their union were easily allayed by her husband's assurance that they were as truly married as it was possible to be in a world without churches or registrars. What she missed far more than certificate or blessing was the paraphernalia and accompanying circumstance of the wedding, to which she had always looked forward as the culminating point of her existence; her veil, her bouquet, her bevy of bridesmaids, her importance! . . . When she sat with her back against a tree-trunk, listlessly unobservant of the play of dappled sunlight or the tracery of leafage, she would crave in the shallows of her disappointed heart for the gaudy little sitting-room that should have been her newly-married dwelling; contrasting its impossible and non-existent splendours with the ramshackle roof-tree under which she took shelter from the weather. The gaudy, tasteless, stuffy little room wherein she should have set out her wedding presents, displayed her photos and done honours of possession to her friends. . . . That was matrimony as she understood it; enhanced importance, display of her matronly dignity. And instead, a marriage that aroused no envy, called forth no jests, affected none but the partners to the bond; in the unchanged discomfort of unchanged surroundings—wherein, being crowd-bred, she could see little beauty and no meaning; in the frequent loneliness and silence abhorrent to her noise-loving soul; with the evening companionship of a wearied man to whom her wifehood meant no more than a physical relation.

Theodore, being male, was not troubled by her abstract longings for the minor dignities of matrimony—and, expecting little from his married life, it could not bring him disillusion. Ada might have fancied that what stirred in her was love; he had always known himself moved by a physical instinct only. Thus of the pair he was the less to be pitied when the increased familiarity of their life in common brought its necessary trouble in the shape of friction—revealing the extent of their unlikeness and even, with time, their antagonism. One of the results of her vague but ever-present sense of grievance, her lasting homesickness for a world that had crumbled, was a lack of interest in the world as it was and a reluctance to adapt herself to an environment altogether hateful; hence, on Theodore's side, a justified annoyance at her continued want of resource and the burdensome stupidity which threw extra labour on himself.

She was a thoroughly helpless woman; helpless after the fashion of the town-bred specialist, the product of division of labour. The country, to her, was a district to drive through in a char-à-banc with convenient halts at public-houses. Having lived all her days as the member of a crowd, she was a creature incomplete and undeveloped; she had schooled with a crowd and worked with it, shared its noise and its ready-made pleasures; it is possible that, till red ruin came, she had conceived of no other existence. . . . Leaving school, she had entered a string factory where she pocketed a fairly comfortable wage in return for the daily and yearly manipulation of a machine devoted to the production of a finer variety of twine. Having learned to handle the machine with ease, life had no more to offer her in the way of education, and development came to a standstill. Her meals, for the most part, she obtained without trouble from factory canteens, cheap restaurants or municipal kitchens; thus her domestic duties were few—the daily smearing of a bedroom (frequently omitted) and the occasional cobbling of a garment, bought ready-made. Her reading, since her schooldays, had consisted of novelettes only, and even to these she was not greatly addicted, preferring, as a rule, a more companionable form of amusement—a party to the pictures, gossip with her girlfriends and flirtations more or less open. At twenty-three (when disaster came) she was a buxom, useless and noisy young woman—good-natured, with the brain of a hen; incapable alike of boiling a potato or feeling an interest in any subject that did not concern her directly.

There were moments when she irritated Theodore intensely by her infantile helplessness and the blunders that resulted therefrom, by her owlish stupidity in the face of the new and unfamiliar. And there were moments when, for that very owlishness, he pitied her with equal intensity, realizing that his own loss, his daily wretchedness, was a small thing indeed beside hers. The ruin of a world could not rob him utterly of his heritage of all the ages; part of that heritage no ruin could touch, since he had treasure stored in his heart and brain for so long as his memory should last. But for Ada, whose world had been a world of cheap finery, of giggling gossip and evenings at the cinema, there remained from the ages— nothing. Gossip and cinemas, flowered hats and ribbon-trimmed camisoles—they had left not a wrack, save regret, for her mind to feed on. . . . As the workings of her vacant little soul were laid bare to him, he understood how dreadful was its plight; how pitiably complete must be the blankness of a life such as hers, bereft of the daily little personal interests wherein had been summed up a world. She—unhandy, unresourceful, superficial—was one of the natural and inevitable products of a mechanical civilization; which, in saving her trouble, had stunted her, interposing itself between primary cause and effect. Bread, to her, was food bought at a counter—not grown with labour in a field; the result not of rain, sun and furrow, but of sixpence handed to a tradesman. And cunning men of science had wrestled with the forces of nature that she might drop a penny in the slot for warmth or suck sweets with her "boy" at the pictures.

He guessed her a creature who had always lived noisily, a babbler whom even his fits of taciturnity would not have daunted had she found much to babble of in the lonely world she shared with him; but, bewildered and awed by it, oppressed by its silence, she found meagre subject-matter for the very small talk which was her only method of expression. Under the peace and vastness of the open sky she was homesick for a life that excluded all vastness and peace; her sorrow's crown of sorrow was a helpless, incessant craving for little meaningless noises and little personal excitements. . . . Sometimes, at night, as they sat by the fire, he would see her face pathetic in its blank dreariness; her eyes wandering from the glow of the fire to the darkness beyond it and back from the darkness to the glow. Endeavouring—(or so he imagined)—to piece together some form of inner life from fragmentary memories of past inanity and aimless, ephemeral happenings!

The sight often moved him to pity; but he cast about in vain for a means of allaying her sodden and persistent discontent. Once or twice he attempted to awaken her interest by explaining, as he would have explained to a child, the movements of nightly familiar stars, the habits of birds or the process of growth in vegetation. These things, as he took care to point out, now concerned her directly, were part of the round of her existence; but the fact had no power to stimulate a mind which had been accustomed to accept, without interest or inquiry, the marvels of mechanical science. She carried over into her new life the same lack of curiosity which had character-ized her dealings with the old; she was no more alive to the present phenomena of the open field than to the past phenomena of the electric switch, the petrol-engine or the gas-meter. . . . And the workings of the gas-meter at least had been pleasant—while the workings of raw nature repelled her. Thus Theodore's only reward for his attempt at education was a bored, inattentive remark, to the effect that she had heard her teacher say something like that at school.

She had all the crowd-liver's horror of her own com-pany; strengthened, in her case, by dislike of her sur-roundings, amounting to abhorrence, and the abiding nervousness that was a natural after-effect of the days when she had fled from her fellows and cowered to the earth in an abject and animal terror. Her unwillingness to let Theodore out of her sight was comprehensible enough, if irritating; but there were times when it was more than irritating—a difficulty added to life. It was impossible to apportion satisfactorily a daily toil that, if Ada had her way, must always be performed in company; while her customary fellowship on his hunting and snaring expedi-tions meant not only the presence of a clumsy idler but the dying down of a neglected log-fire and the postpone-ment of all preparations for a meal until after their return to camp. Further, it was a bar to that wider exploration of the neighbourhood which, as time went on, he desired increasingly; confining him, except on comparatively rare occasions, to such range from his hearthstone as could be attained in the company of Ada. So long as he attributed it to the workings of fear only, he was hopeful that, with time, her abhorrence of loneliness might pass; but as the months went by he realized that it was not only fear that kept her close to his heels—her town-bred incapacity to interest or occupy herself.

Once—when the call of the outside world grew louder—he proposed to Ada that he should see her well provided with a store of food and fuel and leave her for two or three days; hoping to tempt her to agreement by pointing out the probability, amounting to certainty, that other survivors of disaster must be dwelling somewhere within reach. Peaceable survivors with whom they could join forces with advantage. . . . Her face lit up for a moment at the idea of other men's company; but when she understood that he proposed to go alone, her terror at the idea of being left was abject and manifest. She was afraid of everything and anything; of ghosts, of darkness, of prowling men, of spiders and possible snakes; and, having reasoned in vain, in the end he gave her the assurance she clamoured for—that she should not be called on to suffer the agony of a night by herself.

He gave her the promise in sheer pity, but regretted it as soon as made. He had set his heart on a journey in search of the world that gave no sign, planning to undertake it before the days grew shorter; but he did not disguise from himself that there might still be danger in the expedition—which Ada's hampering presence would increase. The project was abandoned for the time being, in the hope that she would see reason later; but he regretted his promise and weakness the more when he found that Ada did not trust to his word and, fearing lest he gave her the slip, now clung to him as closely as his shadow. Her suspicion and stupidity annoyed him; and there were times when he was ashamed of his own irritation when he saw her trotting, like a dog, at his heels or squatting within eyeshot of his movements. He was conscious of a longing to slap her silly face, and more than once he spoke sharply to her, urged her to go home; whereupon she sulked or cried, but continued her trotting and squatting.

The irritation came to a head one afternoon in the early days of autumn when, with persistent ill-luck, he had been fishing a mile or so from home. Various causes combined to bring about the actual outbreak; a growing anxiety with regard to the winter supply of provisions, sharpened by the discovery, the night before, that a considerable proportion of his store of vegetables was a failure and already malodorous; the ill-success of several hours' fishing, and gusty, unpleasant weather that chilled him as he huddled by the water. The weather worsened after midday, the gusts bringing rain in their wake; a cold slanting shower that sent him, in all haste, to the clump of trees where Ada had sheltered since the morning. The sight of her sitting there to keep an eye on him—uselessly watchful and shivering to no purpose—annoyed him suddenly and violently; he turned on her sharply, as the shower passed, and bade her go home on the instant. She was to keep a good fire, a blazing fire—he would be drenched and chilled by the evening. She was to have water boiling that the meal might be cooked the moment he returned with the wherewithal. . . . While he spoke she eyed him with questioning, distrustful sullenness; then, convinced that he meant what he said, half rose—only, after a moment of further hesitation, to slide down to her former position with her back against the trunk of a beech-tree.

"I don't want to," she said doggedly. "I want to stay 'ere. I don't see why I shouldn't. What d'yer want to get rid of me for?"

The suspicion that lay at the back of the refusal infuriated him: it was suddenly intolerable to be followed and spied on, and he lost his temper badly. The rough-tongued vehemence of his anger surprised himself as much as it frightened his wife; he swore at her, threatened to duck her in the stream, and poured out his grievances abusively. What good was she?—a clog on him, who could not even tend a fire, a helpless idiot who had to be waited on, a butter-fingered idler without brains! Let her do what he told her and make herself of use, unless she wanted to be turned out to fend for herself. . . . Much of what he said was justified, but it was put savagely and coarsely; and when—cowed, perhaps, by the suggestion of a ducking—Ada had taken to her heels in tears, he was remorseful as well as surprised at his own vehemence. He had not known himself as a man who could rail brutally and use threats to a woman; the revelation of his new possibilities troubled him; and when, towards sundown, he gathered up his meagre prey and stepped out homeward, it was with the full intention of making amends to Ada for the roughness of his recent outburst.

His path took him through a copse of brushwood into what had been a cart-track; now grass-grown and crumbling between hedges that straggled and encroached. The wind, rising steadily, was sweeping ragged clouds before it and as he emerged from the shelter of the copse he was met by a stinging rain. He bent his head to it, in shivering discomfort, thrusting chilled hands under his cloak for warmth and longing for the blaze and the good warm meal that should thaw them; he had left the copse a good minute behind him when, from the further side of the overgrown hedge, he heard sudden rending of brambles, a thud, and a human cry. A yard or two on was a gap in the hedge where a gate still swung on its hinges; he rushed to it, quivering at the thought of possibilities—and found Ada struggling to her knees!

She began to cry loudly when she saw him, like a child caught in flagrant transgression; protesting, with bawling and angry tears, that "she wasn't going to be ordered about" and "she should staiy just where she liked!" It did not take him long to gather that her previous flight had been a semblance only and that, shivering and haunted by ridiculous suspicion, she had watched him all the afternoon from behind the screen of the copse wood—for company partly, but chiefly to make sure he was there. Seeing him gather up his tackle and depart homeward, she had tried to outpace him unseen; keeping the hedge between them as she ran and hoping to avert a second explosion of his wrath by blowing up the ashes of the fire before his arrival at the camp. An unsuspected rabbit-burrow had tripped her hurrying feet and brought about disaster and discovery; and she made unskilful efforts to turn the misfortune to account by rubbing her leg and complaining of damage sustained.

In contact with her stubborn folly his repentance and kindly resolutions were forgotten; he cut short her bid for sympathy with a curt "Get along with you," caught her by the arm and started her with a push along the road—too angry to notice that, for the first time, he had handled her with actual violence. Then, bending his head to the sweep of the rain, he strode on, leaving her to follow as she would.

Perhaps her leg really pained her, perhaps she judged it best to keep her distance from his wrath; at any rate she was a hundred yards or more behind him when he reached the camp and, stirring the ashes that should have been a fire, found only a flicker alive. He cursed Ada's idiocy between his chattering teeth as he set to work to rekindle the fire; his hands shaking, half from anger, half from cold, as he gathered the fuel together. When, after a long interval of coaxing and cursing, the flame quivered up into the twilight, it showed him Ada sitting humped at the entrance to their shelter; and at sight of her, inert and watching him—watching him!—his wrath flared sudden and furious.

"Have you filled the cookpot?" he asked, standing over her. "No? . . . Then what were you doing—sitting there staring while I worked?"

She began to whimper, "You're crool to me!"—and repeated her parrot-like burden of futile suspicion and grievance; that she knew he wanted to get her out of the way so as he could leave her, and she couldn't be left alone for the night! He had a sense of being smothered by her foolish, invertebrate persistence, and as he caught her by the shoulders he trembled and sputtered with rage.

"God in Heaven, what's the good of talking to you? If you take me for a liar, you take me—that's all. Do you think I care a curse for your opinion? . . . But one thing's certain—you'll do what I tell you, and you'll work. Work, do you hear?—not sit in a lump and idle and stare while I wait on you! Learn to use your silly hands, not expect me to light the fire and feed you. And you'll obey, I tell you— you'll do what you're told. If not—I'll teach you. . . ."

He was wearied, thwarted, wet through and unfed since the morning; baulked of fire and a meal by the folly that had irked him for days; a man living primitively, in contact with nature and brought face to face with the workings of the law of the strongest. It chanced that she had lumped herself down by the bundle of osier-rods he had laid together for his basket-making; so that when he gripped her by the nape of the neck a weapon lay ready to his hand. He used it effectively, while she wriggled, plunged and howled; there was nothing of the Spartan in her temperament, and each swooping stroke produced a yell. He counted a dozen and then dropped her, leaving her to rub and bemoan her smarts while he filled the cookpot at the stream.

When he came back with the cookpot filled, her noisy blubbering had died into gulps and snuffles. The heat of his anger was likewise over, having worked itself off by the mere act of chastisement, and with its cooling he was conscious of a certain embarrassment. If he did not repent he was at least uneasy—not sure how to treat her and speak to her—and he covered his uneasiness, as best he might, by a busy scraping and cleaning of fish and a noisy snapping of firewood. . . . A wiser woman might have guessed his embarrassment from his bearing and movements and known how to wrest an advantage by transforming it into remorse; Ada, sitting huddled and smarting on her moss-bed, found no more effective protest against ill-treatment than a series of unbecoming sniffs. With every silent moment his position grew stronger, hers weaker; unconsciously he sensed her acquiescence in the new and brutal relation, and when—over his shoulder—he bade her "Come along, if you want any supper," he knew, without looking, that she would come at his word, take the food that he gave her and eat.

They discussed the subject once and very briefly—at the latter end of a meal consumed in silence. A full stomach gives courage and confidence; and Ada, having supped and been heartened, tried a sulky "You've been very crool to me."

In answer, she was told, "You deserved it."

After this unpromising beginning it took her two or three minutes to decide on her next observation.

"I believe," she quavered tearfully, "you've taken the skin off my back."

"Nonsense!" he said curtly. Which was true.

The episode marked his acceptance of a new standard, his definite abandonment of the code of civilization in dealings between woman and man. With another wife than Ada the lapse into primitive relations would have been less swift and certainly far less complete; she was so plainly his mental inferior, so plainly amenable to the argument of force and no other, that she facilitated his conversion to the barbaric doctrine of marriage. And his conversion was the more thorough and lasting from the success of his uncivilized methods of ruling a household; where reasoning and kindliness had failed of their purpose, the sting of the rod had worked wonders. . . . Ada sulked through the evening and sniffed herself to sleep; but in the morning, when he woke, she had filled the cookpot and was busied at the breakfast fire.

They had adapted themselves to their environment, the environment of primitive humanity. That morning when he started for his snaring he started alone; Ada stayed, without remonstrance, to dry moss, collect firewood and perform the small duties of the camp.

XIV

It was a solid fact that from the day of her subjection to the rod and rule of her overlord, Ada found life more bearable; and watching her, at first in puzzlement, Theodore came by degrees to understand the reason for the change in her which was induced—so it seemed—by the threat and magic of an osier-wand. In the end he realized that the fundamental cause of her sodden, stupid wretchedness had been lack of effective interest—and that in finding an interest, however humble, she had found herself a place in the world. Her interest, in the beginning, was nothing more exalted than the will to avoid a second switching; but, undignified as it was in its origin, it implied a stimulus to action which had hitherto been wanting, and a process of adaptation to the new relationship between herself and her man. By accepting him as master, with the right unquestioned of reward and punishment, she had provided herself with that object in life to which she had been unable to attain by the light of her own mentality.

With an eye on the osier-heap she worked that she might please and, finding occupation, brooded less; learning imperceptibly to look on the new world primitive as a reality whose hardships could be mitigated by effort, instead of an impossible nightmare. As she wrestled with present difficulties—the daily tasks she dared no longer neglect—the trams, shop-windows and chiffons of the past receded on her mental horizon. Not, fundamentally, that they were any less dear to her; but the need of placating an overlord at hand took up part of her thoughts and time. Too slothful, both in mind and in body, to acquire of her own intelligence and initiative the changed habits demanded by her changed surroundings, she was unconsciously relieved—because instantly more comfortable—when the necessary habits were forced on her.

With the allotment of her duties and the tacit definition of her status that followed on the night of her chastisement, their life on the whole became easier, better regulated; and the mere fact of their frequent separation during part of the day made their coming together more pleasant. Companionship in any but the material sense it was out of her power to offer; but she could give her man a welcome at the end of the day and take lighter work off his hands. Her cooking was always a matter of guesswork and to the last she was stupid, unresourceful and clumsy with her fingers; but she fetched and carried, washed pots and garments in the stream, was hewer of wood and drawer of water and kept their camp clean and in order. In time she even learned to take a certain amount of pleasure in the due fulfilment of her task-work; when Theodore, having discovered a Spanish chestnut-tree not far from their dwelling, set her the job of storing nuts against the winter, she pointed with pride in the evening to the size of the heap she had collected.

Now that she was admittedly his underling, subdued to his authority, he found it infinitely easier to be patient with her many blunders; and though there were still moments when her brainlessness and limitations galled him to anger, on the whole he grew fonder of her—with a patronizing, kindly affection. He still cherished his plans of exploration unhampered by her company but, from pity for the fears she no longer dared to talk of, refrained from present mention thereof; while the nights were long and dark it would be cruel to leave her, and by the time spring came round again she might have grown less fearful of solitude. . . . Or, before spring came, the world might make a sign and plans of exploration be needless.

Meanwhile, resigning himself to his daily and solitary round, he worked hard and anxiously to provision his household for a second winter of loneliness.

It was when the days were nearly at their shortest that the round and tenor of his life was broken by the shock of a disturbing knowledge. Trudging homewards toward sunset on a mild December evening, he came upon his wife sitting groaning in the path; she had been on her way to the stream for water when a paroxysm of sickness overtook her. Since the days of starvation he had never seen her ill and the violence of the paroxysm frightened him; when it was over and she leaned on him exhausted as he led her back to their camping-place, he questioned her anxiously as to what had upset her—had she pain, had she eaten anything unwholesome or unusual? She shook her head silently in answer to his queries till he sat her down by the fire; then, as he knelt beside her, stirring the logs into a blaze, she caught his arm suddenly and pressed her face tightly against it.

"Ow, Theodore, I'm going to 'ave a baiby!"

"What?" he said. "What?"—and stared at her, his mouth wide open. . . . Perhaps she was hurt or disappointed at his manner of taking the news; at any rate she burst into floods of noisy weeping, rocking herself backwards and forwards and hiding her face in her hands. He did his best to soothe her, stroking her hair and encircling her shoulders with an arm; seeking vainly for the words that would stay her tears, for something that would hearten and uplift her. He supposed she was frightened—more frightened even than he was; his first bewildered thought, when he heard the news, had been "What, in God's name, shall we do?"

He drew her head to his shoulder, muttering "There, there," as one would to a child, till her noisy demonstrative sobbing died down to an intermittent whimper; and when she was quieted she volunteered an answer to the question his mind had been forming. She thought it would be somewhere about five months—but it mightn't be so long, she couldn't be sure. She didn't know enough about it to be sure—how could she, seeing as it was her first? . . . She had been afraid for ever so long now—weeks and weeks—but she'd gone on hoping and that was why she hadn't said anything about it before. Now there wasn't any doubt—she wondered he hadn't seen for himself . . .

and she clung to him again with another burst of noisy weeping.

"But," he ventured uncertainly, reaching out after comfort, "when it's over—and there's the baby—you'll be glad, won't you?"

His appeal to the maternal instinct had no immediate success. Ada protested with yet noisier crying that she was bound to die when the baby came, so how could she possibly be glad? It was all very well for him to talk like that—he didn't have to go through it! Lots of women died, even when they had proper 'orspitals and doctors and nurses. . . .

He listened helplessly, not knowing how to take her; until, common sense coming to his aid, he fell back on the certainty that exhausting, hysterical weeping could by no possibility be good for her, rebuked her with authority for upsetting herself and insisted on immediate self-control. It was well for them both that wifely obedience was already a habit with Ada; by the change in his tone she recognized an order, pulled herself together, rubbed her swollen eyes and even made an effort to help with the preparing of supper—whining a little, now and again, but checking the whine before it had risen to a wail.

She was manifestly cheered by a bowlful of hot stew—whereof, though she pushed it away at first, she finished by eating sufficiently; and, once convinced that the outburst of emotion was over, he petted her, though not too sympathetically, lest he stirred her again to self-pity. She was not particularly responsive to his hesitating suggestions anent the coming joys of maternity; more successful in raising her spirits were his actual encouraging pats and caresses, his assumption of confidence greater than he felt in the neighbourhood of men and women whose hands were not turned against their fellows. . . . He realized that, as the suspicion of her motherhood grew to a certainty, she had spent long, lonely hours oppressed by sheer physical terror; and he reproached himself for having been carelessly unobservant of a suffering that should long ere this have been plain to him.

He was longing to be alone and to think undistracted; it was a relief to him therefore when, warmed, fed, and exhausted by her crying, she began to nod against his shoulder. He insisted jestingly on immediate bed, patted and pulled at her moss-couch before she lay down, kissed her—whereupon she again cried a little—and sat beside her, listening, till her breathing was even and regular. Once sure that she slept, he crept back to the fire to sit with his chin on his hands; outside was the silence of a still December night, where the only sound was the rush of water and the hiss and snap of burning logs.

With his elbows on his knees and his chin on his hands, he stared into the fire and the future . . . wondering why it had come as a shock to him—this natural, this almost inevitable consequence of the life he shared with a woman? He found no immediate answer to the question; understanding only that the animal and unreflecting need which had driven them into each other's arms had coloured their whole sex-relation. They had lived like the animal, without any thought of the future. . . . Now the civilized man in him demanded that his child should be born of something more than unreasoning lust of the flesh and there stirred in him a craving to reverence the mother of his son. . . . Ada, flaccid, lazy, infantile of mind, was more, for the moment, than her prosaic, incapable self. A rush of tenderness swept over him—for her and for the little insistent life which might, when its time came, have to struggle into being unaided. . . .

With the thought returned the dread which had flashed into his mind when Ada revealed to him his fatherhood. If their life in hiding were destined to continue—if all men within reach were as those they had fled from, there would come the moment when—he should not know what to do! . . . He remembered, years ago, in the rooms of a friend, a medical student, how, with prurient youthful curiosity, he had picked up a textbook on midwifery—and sought feverishly to recall what he had read as he fluttered its pages and eyed its startling illustrations.

As had happened sometimes in the first days of loneliness, the immensity of the world overwhelmed him; he sat crouched by his fire, an insect of a man, surrounded by unending distances. An insect of a man, a pigmy, whom nature in her vastness ignored; yet, for all his insignificance, the guardian of life, the keeper of a woman and her child. . . . They would look to him for sustenance, for guidance and protection; and he, the little man, would fend for them—his mate and his young. . . .

Of a sudden he knew himself close kin to the bird and beast; to the buck-rabbit diving to the burrow where his doe lay cuddled with her soft blind babies; to the round-eyed blackbird with a beakful gathered for the nest. . . . The loving, anxious, protective life of the winged and furry little fathers—its unconscious sacrifice brought a lump to his throat and the world was less alien and dreadful because peopled with his brethren—the guardians of their mates and their young.

XV

It was clear to him, so soon as he knew of his coming fatherhood, that, in spite of the drawbacks of winter travelling, his long-deferred journey of exploration must be undertaken at once; the companionship of men, and above all of women, was a necessity to be sought at the risk of any peril or hardship. Hence—with misgiving—he broached the subject to Ada next morning; and in the end, with smaller opposition than he had looked for, her lesser fears were mastered by her greater. That the certain future danger of unaided childbirth might be spared her, she consented to the present misery of days and nights of solitude; and together they made preparations for his voyage of discovery in the outside world and her lonely sojourn in the camp.

As he had expected, her first suggestion had been that they should break camp and journey forth together; but he had argued her firmly out of the idea, insisting less on the possible dangers of his journey—which he strove, rather, to disguise from her—than on her own manifest unfitness for exertion and exposure to December weather. Once more the habit of wifely obedience came to his assistance and her own, and she bowed to her overlord's decision—if tearfully, without temper or sullenness; while, the decision once taken, it was he, and not

Ada, who lay wakeful through the night and conjured up visions of possible disaster in his absence. His imagination was quickened by the new, strange knowledge of his responsibility, the protective sense it had awakened; and, lying wide awake in the still of the night, it was not only possible danger to Ada that he dreaded—he was suddenly afraid for himself. If misfortune befell him on his journey into the unknown, it would be more than his own misfortune; on his strength, his luck and well-being depended the life of his woman and her unborn child. If evil befell him and he never came back to them—if he left his bones in the beyond. . . . At the thought the sweat broke out on his face and he started up shivering on his moss-bed.

He worked through the day at preparations for the morning's departure which, if simple, demanded thought and time; saw that plentiful provision of food and dry fuel lay ready to his wife's hand, so that small exertion would be needed for the making of fire and meal. For his own provisioning he filled a bag with cooked fish, chestnuts and the like—store enough to keep him with care for five or six days. All was made ready by nightfall for an early start on the morrow; and he was awake and afoot with the first reddening of a dull December morning. Fearing a breakdown from Ada at the last moment, he had planned to leave her still asleep; but the crackling of a log he had thrown on the embers roused her and she sat up, pushing the tumbled brown hair from her eyes.

"You're gowing?" she asked with a catch in her voice; and he avoided her eye as he nodded back "Yes," and slung his bag over his shoulder.

"Just off," he told her with blatant cheeriness. "Take care of yourself and have a good breakfast. There's water in the cookpot—and mind you look after the fire. I've put you plenty of logs handy—more than you'll want till I come back. Good-bye!"

"You might say good-bye properly," she whimpered after him.

He affected not to hear and strode away whistling; he had purposely tried to make the parting as careless and unemotional as his daily going forth to work. Purposely, therefore, he did not look back until he was too far away to see her face; it was only when the trees were about to hide him that he turned, waved and shouted and saw her lift an arm in reply. She did not shout back—he guessed that she could not—and when the trees hid him he ran for a space, lest the temptation to follow and call him back should master her.

He had planned out his journey often enough during the last few months; considering the drift of the river and lie of the country and attempting to reduce them to map-form on the soil by the aid of a pointed stick. His idea was to make, in the first place, for the silent village which had hitherto been the limit of his voyaging; and thence to follow the road beside the river which in time, very surely, must bring him to the haunts of men. Somewhere on the banks of the river—beyond the tract of devastated ground—must dwell those who drank from its waters and fished in them; who perhaps—now the night of destruction was over and humanity had ceased to tear at and prey upon itself—were rebuilding their civilization and salving their treasures from ruin! . . . The air, crisp and frosty, set him walking eagerly, and as his body glowed from the swiftness of his pace a pleasurable excitement took hold of him; his sweating fears of the night were forgotten and his brain worked keenly, adventurously. Somewhere, and not far, were men like unto himself, beginning their life and their world anew in communities reviving and hopeful. Even, it might be—(he began to dream dreams)—communities comparatively unscathed; with homes and lands unpoisoned, unshattered, living ordered and orderly lives! . . . Some such communities the devils of destruction must have spared . . . if a turn in the valley should reveal to him suddenly a town like the old towns, with men going out and in!

He quickened his pace at the thought and the miles went under him happily. He was no longer alone; even when he entered the long waste of coarse grass and blackened tree that lay around the dead village its dreariness was peopled with his vivid and hopeful imaginings . . . of a crowd that hustled to hear his story, that questioned and welcomed and was friendly—and led him to a house that was furnished and whole . . . where were books and good comfort and talk. . . .

So, in pleasant company, he trudged until well after midday; when, perhaps discouraged by the beginnings of bodily weariness, perhaps affected by the sight of the stark village street—his unreasonable hopefulness passed and anxiety returned. He grew conscious, suddenly and acutely, of his actual surroundings; of silence, of the waste he had trodden, of the desolation about him, of the unknown loneliness ahead. That above all— the indefinite, on-stretching loneliness. . . . He hurried through the dumb street nervously, listening to his own footsteps—the beat and the crunch of them on a frozen road, their echo against deserted walls; and at the end of the village he turned with relief into the road he had marked on his previous visit, the road that turned to run by the stream a few yards beyond the bridge. It wound dismally into a scorched little wood—not one live shoot in it, a cemetery of poisoned trees; then on, still keeping fairly close to the stream, through the same long waste patched with grass and spreading weed. The road, though it narrowed and was overgrown and crumbling in places, was easy enough to follow for the first few hours, but he sought in vain for traces of its recent use. There was no sign of man or the works of man in use; the only token of his presence were, now and again, a fire-blackened cottage, a jumble of rusted, twisted ironwork or a skeleton with rank grass thrusting through the whitened ribs. When the river rounded a turn in the hills, the prospect before him was even as the prospect behind; a waste and silence where corn had once grown and cattle pastured.

As the day wore on the heavy silence was irksome and more than irksome. It was broken only by the sound of his footsteps, the whisper of grass in a faint little wind and now and again—more rarely—by the chirp and flutter of a bird. Long before dusk he began to fear the night, to think, with something like craving, of the shelter and the fire and the woman beside it—that was home; the thought of hours of darkness spent alone amongst the whitened bones of men and the blackened carcases of trees loomed before him as a growing threat. He pushed on doggedly, refusing himself the spell of rest he needed, in the hope that when night came down on him he might have left the drear wilderness behind.

It was a hope doomed to disappointment; the fall of the early December evening found him still in the unending waste, and when the dusk thickened into darkness he camped, perforce, near the edge of the river in the lee of a broken wall. The branches of a dead tree near by afforded him fuel for the fire that he kindled with difficulty with the aid of a rough contrivance of flint and steel; and as he crouched by the blaze and ate his evening ration he scanned the night sky with anxious and observant eyes. So far the weather had been clear and dry, but he realized the peril of a break in it, of a snowstorm in shelterless country. . . . If to-morrow were only as to-day—if the waste stretched on without trace of man or sign of ending—what then? Would it be wise or safe to push on for yet another day—leaving home yet further behind him? For the journey back the waste must be recrossed, in whatever weather the winter pleased to send him; traversed by day and camped on by night, in hail, in rain, in snow. . . . The thought gave him pause since exposure might well mean death—and to more than himself.

He slept little and brokenly, rousing at intervals with a shiver as the fire died down for want of tendance; and was on his feet with the first grey of morning, trudging forward with fear at his heels. It was a fear that pressed close on them with the passing of long lonely hours; still wintry hours wherethrough he strained his eyes for a curl of smoke or a movement on the outspread landscape. . . . The day was yesterday over again; the same pale sky, the dull swollen river that led him on, and the endless waste of shallow valley; and when night came down again he knew only this—a clump of hills that had been distant was nearer, and he was a day's tramp further on his way. He settled at sundown in a copse of withered trees which afforded him plentiful firing if little else in the way of shelter from the night; and having kindled a blaze he warmed his food, ate and slept—too weary to lie awake and brood.

He had not slept long—for the logs still glowed redly and flickered—when he started into wakefulness that was instant, complete and alert. Something—he knew it—had stirred in the silence and roused him; he sat up, peered round and listened with the watchful terror instinctive in the hunted, be the hunted beast or man. For a moment he peered round, seeing nothing, hearing nothing but the whisper of the fire and the beating of his own heart . . . then, in the blackness, two points caught the firelight— eyes! . . . Eyes unmistakable, that glowed and were fixed on him. . . .

He stiffened and stared at them, open-mouthed; then, as a sudden flicker of the dying flame showed the out- line of a bearded human face, he choked out something inarticulate and made to scramble to his feet. Swift as was the movement he was still on a knee when someone from behind leaped on him and pinned both arms to his sides. . . . As he wrestled instinctively other hands grasped him; he was the held and helpless captive of three or four who clutched him by throat, wrist and shoulder. . . .

By that token he was back among men.

XVI

When they had him down and helpless at their feet, a dry branch was thrust into the embers and, as it flamed, held aloft that the light might fall upon his face. To him it revealed the half-dozen faces that looked down at him— weatherworn, hairy and browned with dirt, the eyes, for the moment, aglow with the pleasure of the hunter who has tracked and snared his prey. They held their prey and gazed at it, as they would have gazed at and measured a beast they had roped into helplessness. Satisfaction at the capture shone in their faces; the natural and grim satisfaction of him who has met and mastered his natural enemy. . . . That, for the moment, was all; they had met with a man and overcome him. Curiosity, even, would come later.

Theodore, after his first instinctive lunge and struggle, lay motionless—flaccid and beaten; understanding in a flash that was agony that men were still what they had been when he fled from them into the wilderness—beast-men who stalked and tore each other. In the torchlight the dirty, coarse faces were savage and animal; the eyes that glowered down at him had the staring intentness of the animal. . . . He expected death from a blow or a knife-thrust, and closed his eyes that he might not see it coming; and instead saw, as plainly as with bodily eyes, a vision of Ada by the camp fire, sitting hunched and listening for his footstep. Listening for it, staring at the dreadful darkness—through night after dreadful night. . . . In a torment of pity for his mate and her child he stammered an appeal for his life.

"For God's sake—I wasn't doing any harm. If you'll only listen—my wife. . . . All that I want. . . ."

If they were moved they did not show it, and it may be they were not moved—having lived, themselves, through so much of misery and bodily terror that they had ceased to respond to its familiar workings in others. Fear and the expression of fear to them were usual and normal, and they listened undisturbed while he tried to stammer out his pleading. Not only undisturbed but apparently uninterested; while he spoke one was twisting the knife from his belt and another taking stock of the contents of his food-bag; and he had only gasped out a broken sentence or two when the holder of the torch—as it seemed the leader—cut him short with "Are you alone?" . . . Once satisfied on that head he listened no more, but dropped the torch back on to the fire and kicked apart the dying embers. The action was apparently a sign to move on; the hands that gripped Theodore dragged him to his feet and urged him forward; and, with a captor holding to either arm, he stumbled out of the clump of stark trees into the open desert—now whitened by a moon at the full.

There was little enough talk amongst his captors as, for more than two hours, they thrust and guided him along; such muttered talk as there was, was not addressed to their prisoner and he judged it best to be silent. It was—so he guessed—the red shine of his fire that had drawn attention to his presence; and, the fear of instant death removed, he drew courage from the thought that the men who held and hurried him must be dwellers in some near-by village. Once he had reached it and been given opportunity to tell his story and explain his presence, they would cease to hold him in suspicion—so he comforted himself as they strode through the wilderness in silence.

After an hour of steady tramping they turned inland sharply from the river till a mile or so brought them to broken, rising ground and a smaller stream babbling from the hills. They followed its course, for the most part steadily uphill, and, at the end of another mile, the scorched black stumps gave place to trees uninjured— spruce firs in their solemn foliage and oaks with their tracery of twigs. A copse, then a stretch of short turf and the spring of heather underfoot; then down, to more trees growing thickly in a hollow—and through them a glow that was fire. Then figures that moved, silhouetted, in and out of the glow and across it; an open space in the midst of the trees and hut-shapes, half-seen and half-guessed at, in the mingling of flicker and deep shadow. . . . Out of the darkness a dog yapped his warning—then another—and at the sound Theodore thrilled and quivered as at a voice from another world. Now and again, while he lived in his wilderness, he had heard the sharp and familiar yelp of some masterless dog, run wild and hunting for his food; but the dog that lived with man and guarded him was an adjunct of civilization!

The warning had roused the little community before the newcomers emerged from the shadow of the trees; and as they entered the clearing and were visible, men hurried towards them, shouting questions. Theodore found himself the centre of a staring, hustling group— which urged him to the fire that it might see him the better, which questioned his guards while it stared at him. . . . Here, too, was the strange aloofness that refrained from direct address; he was gazed at, stolidly or eagerly, taken stock of as if he were a beast, and his guards explained how and where they had found him, as if he himself were incapable of speech, as they might have spoken of the finding of a dog that had strayed from its owner. Perhaps it was uneasiness that held him silent, or perhaps he adapted himself unconsciously to the general attitude; at any rate—as he remembered afterwards—he made no effort to speak.

The men and women who crowded round him, staring and murmuring, were in number, perhaps, between thirty and forty; women with matted hair straggling and men unshorn, their garments, like his own, a patchwork of oddments and all of them uncouth and unclean. One woman, he noted, had a child at her half-naked breast; a dirty little nursling but a few months old, its downy pate crusted with scabs. He stared at it, wondering as to the manner of its birth—the mother returning his scrutiny with open-mouthed interest until shouldered aside without ceremony by a man whom Theodore recognized for the leader of his band of captors. When they reached the shadow of the clump of trees he had stridden ahead and vanished, presumably to report and seek orders from some higher authority; and now, at a word from him, Theodore was again jerked forward by his guards and, with the crowd breaking and trailing behind him, was led some fifty or sixty yards further to where, on the edge of the clump of trees, stood a building, a tumbledown cottage. The moon without and a fire within showed broken panes stuffed with moss and a thatched roof falling to decay; inside the atmosphere was foul and stale, and heavy with the heat of a blazing wood fire which alone gave light to the room.

By the fire, seated on a backless kitchen chair, sat a man, grey of head and bent of shoulder; but even in the firelight his eyes were keen and steely—large bright-blue eyes that shone under thick grey eyebrows. His face, with its bright, stubborn eyes and tight mouth, was—for all its dirt—the face of a man who gave orders; and it did not escape the prisoner that the others—the crowd that was thrusting and packing itself into the room—were one and all silent till he spoke.

"Come nearer," he said—and on the word, Theodore was pushed close to him. "Let him go"—and Theodore was loosed. Someone, at a sign, lit a stick from the heap beside the fire and held it aloft; and for a moment, till it flared itself out, there was silence, while the old man peered at the stranger. With the sudden light the hustling and jostling ceased, and the crowd, like Theodore, waited on the old man's words.

"Tell me," at last came the order, "what you were doing here. Tell me everything"—and he lifted a dirty lean finger like a threat—"what you were doing on our land, where you came from, what you want? . . . and speak the truth or it will be the worse for you."

Theodore told him; while the steel-blue eyes searched his face as well as they might in the semi-darkness and the half-seen crowd stood mute. He told of his life as it had been lived with Ada; of their complete separation from their fellows for the space of nearly two years; of the coming of the child and the consequent need of help for his wife—conscious, all the time, not only of the questioning, unshrinking eyes of his judge but of the other eyes that watched him suspiciously from the corners and shadows of the room. Two or three times he faltered in his telling, oppressed by the long, steady silence; for throughout there was no comment, no word of interest or encouragement—only once, when he paused in the hope of encouragement, the old man ordered "Go on!" . . . He went on, striving to steady his voice and pleading against he knew not what of hostility, suspicion and fear.

". . . And so," he ended uncertainly, "they found me. I wasn't doing any harm. . . . I suppose they saw my fire? . . ."

From someone in the darkness behind him came a grunt that might indicate assent—then, again, there was silence that lasted. . . . The dumb, heavy threat of it was suddenly intolerable and Theodore broke it with vehemence.

"For God's sake tell me what you're going to do! It's not much I ask and it's not for myself I ask it. If you can't help me yourselves there must be other people who can—tell me where I am and where I ought to go. My wife—she must have help."

There was no actual response to his outburst, but some of the half-seen figures stirred and he heard a muttering in the shadow that he took for the voices of women.

"Tell me where I am," he repeated, "and where I can go for help."

It was the first question only that was answered.

"You are on our land."

"Your land—but where is it? In what part of England?"

"I don't know," said the old man and shrugged his lean shoulders. "But you haven't any right on it. It's ours."

He pushed back his chair and stood up to his full, tall height; then, raising his hand, addressed the assembly of his followers.

"You have all of you heard what he said and know what he wants. Now let me hear what you think. Say it out loud and not in each other's ears."

He dropped his arm and stood waiting a reply—and after a moment one came from the back of the room.

"It's winter," said a man's voice, half-sulky, half-defiant, "and we've hardly enough left for ourselves. We don't want any more mouths here—we've more than we can fill as it is." A murmur of agreement encouraged him and he went on—louder and pushing through the crowd as he spoke. "We fend for our own and he must fend for his. He ought to think himself lucky if we let him go after we've taken him on our land. What business had he there?"

This time the murmur of agreement was stronger and a second voice called over it:

"If we catch him here again he won't get off so easily!"

The assent that followed was more than assent; applause that swelled and grew almost clamorous. The old man stilled it with a lifting of his knotted hand.

"Then you won't have him here? You don't want him?"

The "No" in answer was vigorous; refusal, it seemed, was unanimous. Theodore tried to speak, to explain that all he asked . . . but again the knotted hand was lifted.

"And are you—for letting him go?"

The words dropped out slowly and were followed by a hush—significant as the question itself. . . . This much was clear to the listener: that behind them lay a fear and a threat. The nature of the threat could be guessed at—since they would not keep him and dared not let him go; but where and what was the motive for the fear that had prompted the slow, sly question and the uneasy silence that followed it? . . . He heard his own heart-beats in the long uneasy silence—while he sought in vain for the reason of their dread of one man and tried in vain to find words. It seemed minutes—long minutes—and not seconds till a voice made answer from the shadows:

"Not if it isn't safe."

And at the words, as a signal, came voices from this side and that—speech hurried, excited and tumultuous. It wasn't safe—what did they know of him and how could they prove his story true? He might be a spy—now he knew where to find them, knew they had food, he might come back and bring others with him! When he tried to speak the voices grew louder, over-shouted him—and one man at his side, gesticulating wildly, cried out that they would be mad to let him go, since they could not tell how much he knew. The phrase was taken up, as it seemed in panic—by man after man and woman after woman—they could not tell how much he knew! They pressed nearer as they shouted, their faces closing in on him—spitting, working mouths and angry eyes. They were handling him almost; and when once they handled him—he knew it—the end would be sure and swift. He dared not move, lest fingers went up to his throat. He dared not even cry out.

It was the old man who saved him with another call for silence. Not out of mercy—there was small mercy in the lined, dirty face—but because, it seemed, there was yet another point to be considered.

"If they came again"—he jerked his head towards the open—"we should be a man the stronger. Now they are stronger than we are—by nearly a dozen. . . ."

Apparently the argument had weight, for its hearers stood uncertain and arrested—and instinct bade Theodore seize on the moment they had given him. . . . What he said in the beginning he could not remember—how he caught their attention and held it—but when cooler consciousness returned to him they were listening while he bargained for his life. . . . He bargained and haggled for the right to live—offering goods and sweat and muscle in exchange for a place on the earth. He was strong and would work for them; he could hunt and fish and dig; he would earn by his labour every mouthful that fell to him, every mouthful that fell to his wife. . . . More, he had food of his own laid away for the winter months—dried fish and nuts and the store of fruit he had salved and hoarded from the autumn. These all could be fetched and shared if need be. . . . He bribed them while they haggled with their eyes. Let them come with him—any of them—and prove what he said; he had more than enough—let them come with him. . . . When he stopped, exhausted and sobbing for breath, the extreme of the danger had passed.

"If he has food," someone grunted—and Theodore, turning to the unseen speaker, cried out—"I swear I have! I swear it!"

He hoped he had won; and then knew himself in peril again when the man who had raised the cry before repeated doggedly that they could not tell how much he knew. . . .

"Take him away," said the old man suddenly. "You take him—you two"—and he pointed twice. "Keep him while we talk—till I send for you."

At least it was reprieve and Theodore knew himself in safety, if only for a passing moment. For their own comfort, if not for his, his guards escorted him to the fire in the open, where they crouched down, stolid and watchful, Theodore between them—exhausted by emotion and flaccid both in body and mind. . . . There was a curious relief in the knowledge that he had shot his last bolt and could do nothing more to save himself; that whatever befell him—release or swift death—was a happening beyond his control. No effort more was required of him and all that he could do was to wait.

He waited dumbly, in the end almost drowsily, with his head bent forward on his knees.

XVII

After minutes, or hours, a hand was laid on his shoulder and shook it; he raised his eyes stupidly, saw his guards already on their feet and with them a third man—sent, doubtless, with orders to summon them. He rose, knowing that a decision had been made, one way or another, but still oddly numb and unmoved. . . . The two men with him thrust a way into the crowded little room, elbowing their fellows aside till they had pushed and dragged their charge to the neighbourhood of the fireplace and set him face to face with his judge. As they fell back a pace or two—as far as the crowding of the room allowed— someone again lit a branch at the fire and held it up that the light might fall upon the prisoner.

To Theodore the action brought with it a conviction that his sentence was death and his manner of receiving it a diversion for the eyes of the beholders. . . . The old man was waiting, intent, with his chin on his hand, that he might lengthen the diversion by lengthening the suspense of the prisoner. . . .

When he spoke at last his words were a surprise— instead of a judgment, came a query.

"What were you?" he asked suddenly; and, at the unexpected, irrelevant question, Theodore, still numb, hesitated—then repeated mechanically, "What was I?"

"In the days before the Ruin—what were you? What sort of work did you do? How did you earn your living?"

He knew that, pointless as the question seemed, there was something that mattered behind it; his face was being searched for the truth and the ring of listeners had ceased to jostle and were waiting in silence for the answer.

"I—I was a clerk," he stammered, bewildered.

"A clerk," the other repeated—as it seemed to Theodore suspiciously. "There were a great many different kinds of clerks—they did all sorts of things. What did you do?"

"I was a civil servant," Theodore explained. "A clerk in the Distribution Office—in Whitehall."

"That means you wrote letters—did accounts?"

"Yes. Wrote letters, principally . . . and filed them. And drew up reports. . . ."

The question sent him back through the ages. In the eye of his mind he saw his daily office—the shelves, the rows of files, interminable files—and himself, neat-suited, clean-fingered, at his desk. Neat-suited, clean-fingered and idling through a short day's work; with Cassidy's head at the desk by the window—and Birnbaum, the Jew boy, who always wore a buttonhole. . . . He brought himself back with an effort, from then to now—from the seemly remembrance of the life bureaucratic to a crowd of evil-smelling savages. . . .

"You were always that—just a clerk? You have never had any other way of earning a living?" . . . And again he knew that the answer mattered, that his "No!" was listened for intently.

"You weren't ever an engineer?" the old man persisted. "Or a scientific man of any kind?"

"No," Theodore repeated, "I have never had anything to do with either engineering or science. When I left the University I went straight into the Distribution Office and I stayed there till the war."

"University!" The word (so it seemed to him) was snatched at. "You're a college man?"

"I was at Oxford," Theodore told him.

"A college man—then they must have taught you science. They always taught it at colleges. Chemistry and that sort of thing—you know chemistry?"

In the crowd was a sudden thrill that was almost murmur; and Theodore hesitated before he answered, his tongue grown dry in his mouth. . . . Were these people, these outcasts from civilization, hoping to find in him a guide and saviour who should lighten the burden of their barbarism by leading them back to the science which had once been a part of their daily life, but of which they had no practical knowledge? . . . If so, how far was it safe to lie to them? and how far, having lied, could he disguise his dire ignorance of processes mechanical and chemical? What would they hope from him, expect in the way of achievement and proof? . . . Miracles, perhaps—sheer blank impossibilities. . . .

"Science—they taught it you," the old man was reiterating, insisting.

"Yes, they taught it me," he stammered, delaying his answer. "That is to say, I used to attend lectures. . . ."

"Then you know chemistry? Gases and how to make them? . . . And machines—do you know about machines? You could help us with machines—tell us how to make one?"

The dirty old face peered up at him, waiting for his "Yes"; and he knew the other faces that he could not see were peering from the shadow with the same odd, sinister eagerness. All waiting, expectant. . . . The temptation to lie was overwhelming and what held him back was no scruple of conscience but the brute impossibility of making good his claim to a knowledge he did not possess. The utter ignorance betrayed by the form of the old man's speech—"You know chemistry—do you know about machines?"—would make no allowance for the difficulty of applying knowledge and see no difference between theory and instant practice. . . . In his hopelessness he gave them the truth and the truth only.

"I have told you already I am not an engineer—I have never had any training in mechanics. As for chemistry—I had to attend lectures at school and college. But that was all—I never really studied it and I'm afraid I remember very little—almost nothing that would be of any practical use to you. . . . I don't know what you want but, whatever it is, it would need some sort of apparatus—a chemist has to have his tools like other men. Even if I were a trained chemist I should need those—even if I were a trained chemist I couldn't separate gases with my bare hands. For that sort of thing you need a laboratory—a workshop—the proper appliances. . . . I'll work for you in any way that's possible—any way—but you mustn't expect impossibilities, chemistry and mechanics from a man who hasn't been trained in them. . . . And why should you expect me to do what you can't do yourselves—why should you? Is it fair? . . ."

There was no immediate answer, but suddenly he knew that the silence around him had ceased to be threatening and tense. The old man's eyes had left his own; they were moving round the room and searching, as it seemed, for assent. . . . In the end they came back to Theodore—and judgment was given.

"If you are what you say you are, we will take you; but if you have lied to us and you know what is forbidden, we shall find you out sooner or later and, as sure as you stand there, we will kill you. If you are what you say you are—a plain man like us and without devil's knowledge—you may come to us and bring your woman, if she also is without devil's knowledge. That is, if you can feed her; we have only enough for ourselves. And from this day forward you will be our man; and to-morrow you will take the oath to be what we are and live as we do, and be our man against all our enemies and perils. Are you agreed to that?"

He was saved and Ada with him—so much he knew; but as yet it was not clear what had saved him. He was to be their man—take an oath and be one with them— and there was the phrase "devil's knowledge," twice repeated. . . . He stared stupidly at the man who had granted his life—realizing that his ordeal was over only when the packed room emptied itself and the old man turned back to his fire.

XVIII

It was the phrase "devil's knowledge" that, when his first bewilderment was over, gave Theodore the clue to the meaning of the scene he had lived through and the outlook of those whose man he would become on the morrow. That and the sudden memory of Markham . . . on the crest of the centuries, on the night when the crest curled over . . .

He was so far taken into tribal fellowship that he had ceased to be openly a prisoner; but the two men who, for the rest of the night, shared with him the shelter of a lean-to hut, took care to bestow themselves between their guest and the entrance. He got little out of them in the way of enlightenment, for they were asleep almost as they flung themselves down on their moss; but for hours, while they snored, Theodore lay open-eyed, piecing together his fragmentary information of the world into which he had strayed.

"Without devil's knowledge"—that, if he understood aright, was the qualification for admission to the life that had survived disaster. "Devil's knowledge" being—if he was not mad—the scientific, mechanical, engineering lore which was the everyday acquirement of thousands on thousands of ordinary civilized men. The everyday acquirements of ordinary men were anathema; if he was not mad, his own life had been granted him for the reason only that he was unskilled and devoid of them. Ignorant, even as the men who spared him, of practical science and mechanics—a plain man, like unto them. . . . Ignorance was prized here, esteemed as a virtue—the old man's query, "You're a college man?" had been accusation disguised.

In a flash it was clear to him, and he saw through the farce whereby he had been tested and tempted; understood the motive that had prompted its cruel low cunning and all that the cunning implied of acceptance of barbarism, insistence on it. . . . What these outcasts, these remnants of humanity feared above all things was a revival of the science, the mechanical powers, that had wrecked their cities, their houses and their lives and made them—what they were. . . . In knowledge was death and in ignorance alone was a measure of peace and security; hence, fearing lest he was of those who knew too much, they had tempted him to confess to forbidden knowledge, to boast of it—that, having boasted, they might kill him without mercy, make an end of his wits with his life. In the torments inflicted by science destructive they had turned upon science and renounced it; and, that their terrors might not be renewed in the future, they were setting up against it an impassable barrier of ignorance. They had put devil's knowledge behind them—with intention for ever. . . . If when they questioned him and led him on, he had yielded to the natural impulse to lie, they would have knocked him on the head—like vermin—without scruple; and the sweat broke out on him as he remembered how nearly he had lied. . . .

He sat up, sweating and staring at darkness, and thrust back the hair from his forehead. . . . He was back among men—who, of set purpose and deliberately, had turned their faces from the knowledge their fathers had acquired by the patience and toil of generations! Who, of set purpose and deliberately, sought to filch from their children the heritage of the ages, the treasure of the mind of man! . . . That was what it meant—the treasure of the mind of man! Renunciation of all that long generations had striven for with patience and learning and devotion. . . . The impossibility and the treason of it—to know nothing, to forget all their fathers had won for them. . . . He remembered old talk of education as a birthright and the agitations of reformers and political parties. To this end.

Who were they, he asked himself, these people who had made a decision so terrible—what manner of men in the old life? Now they were seeking to live as the beasts live, and not only the world material had died to them, but the world of human aspiration. . . . To this they had come, these people who once were human—the beast in them had conquered the brain . . . and like fire there blazed into his brain the commandment: "Thou shalt not eat of the fruit of the Tree of Knowledge! Thou shalt not eat . . . lest ye die."

The command, the prohibition, had suddenly a new significance. Was this, then, the purport of a legend hitherto meaningless? Was this the truth behind the childish symbol? The deadly truth that knowledge is power of destruction—power of destruction too great for the human, the fallible, to wield? . . . Odd that he had never thought of it before—that, familiar all his life with a deadly truth, he had read it as primitive childishness!

"Of the Tree of the Knowledge of good and evil thou shalt not eat . . . lest ye die. . . ."

He sat numbly repeating the words half aloud till there flashed into his brain a memory, a vision of Markham. In his room off Great Smith Street on the night when war was declared—talking rapidly with his mouth full of biscuit. "Only one thing I'm fairly certain about—I ought to have been strangled at birth. . . . If the human animal must fight, it should kill off its scientific men. Stamp out the race of 'em!" . . . What was that but a paraphrase, a modern application of the command laid upon Adam. "Of the Tree of the Knowledge of good and evil thou shalt not eat . . . lest ye die."

To his first impulse—of amazement and shrinking, as from treason—succeeded understanding of the outlook of these men and their decision. More, he wondered why, even in the worst of his despair, he had always believed in the persistence, the re-birth, of the civilization that had bred him. . . . These people—he saw it—were logical, as Markham had been logical—were wise after the event as Markham had been wise before it; and it amazed him that in his porings and guessings at a world reviving he had never hit upon their simple solution of the eternal problem of war. Markham's solution; which, till this moment, he had not taken literally. . . . "You can't combine the practice of science and the art of war; in the end it's one or the other. We, I think, are going to prove that—very definitely." One or the other. The fighting instinct or knowledge!

Man, because he fights, must deny himself knowledge—which is power over the forces of nature; the secrets of nature must be veiled from him by his own ignorance—lest, when the impulse to strife wells up in him, they serve him for infinite destruction. These renegades, in agony, had made confession of their sin, of the corporate sin of a world; had faced the brutality of their own nature; had denied themselves the fruit of the Tree of Knowledge, and led themselves out of temptation. Since fight they must, being men with men's passions, they would limit their powers of destruction. . . . So he read their strange self-denying ordinance.

The thought led him on to wonder whether they were alone in their self-denying ordinance. . . . Surely not—unless they lived hidden, in complete isolation, out of contact with others of their kind. And obviously they did not live isolated; they had spoken of others who were stronger, and of land that was theirs—implying a system of boundary and penalty for trespass and theft. Further, the phrase "against all enemies" indicated at least a possibility of the contact that was bloodshed—yet enemies who had not renounced the advantage of mechanical and scientific knowledge would be enemies who could overwhelm at the first encounter a community fighting as barbarians. . . . What, then, was their relation to a world more civilized and communities that had not renounced? . . .

In the end, from sheer exhaustion, he ceased to sur-mise and argue with himself—and slept suddenly and heavily, huddling for warmth on his moss-bed against the body of his nearest gaoler.

It was a thrust from a foot that awakened him, and he crawled out shivering into the half-light of dawn and the chill of a frostbitten morning; the camp was alive and emerging from its shelters, the women already occu-pied in cooking the morning meal. Theodore and his guardians shared a bowl of steaming mess; a mingling of potatoes, dried greenstuff and gobbets of meat which he guessed to be rat-flesh. They shared it wolfishly, each man eating fast lest his fellows had more than their por-tion; the meal over, the bowl was flung back to the women for washing, and his gaolers—his mates now—relaxed; there was no further reason for unfriendliness and they were willing enough to be communicative, with the slow uncommunicativeness of men who have little but their daily round to talk about.

They had neighbours, yes—at least what you might call neighbours; there was a settlement, much the same size as their own, some three or four hours' journey away, on the other side of the river—that was the nearest, and the tribesmen met sometimes but not often. Being ques-tioned, they explained that there was frequent trouble about fishing rights—where our stretch of river ended and theirs began; trouble and, now and then, fighting. Yes, of course, they lived as we do—how else should they live? . . . They were better off for shelter, having taken possession of a village—but we, in the hills, were much safer, not so easy to attack or surprise. . . . No, they were not the only ones; on this side the river, but farther away, was another settlement, a larger one; there had been trouble with them, too, as they were very short of food and sent out raiding parties. They had fallen on the village across the water, carried off some of its winter stock and set light to three or four houses; later—a month ago—they had fallen on us, less successfully because we were warned and on the look-out for them. . . . That was why we always have watchers at night—the watchers who saw your fire. . . .

Even from a first halting conversation with men who found anything but sheer statement of fact a difficulty, Theodore was able to construct in outline the common life of this new humanity, its politics, internal and external. The constitution of the tribe—the origin and keystone of the social system—had been, in the beginning, as much a matter of reckless chance as the mating of himself and Ada; small wandering groups of men, who had come alive through the agony of war and famine, had been knit together by a common need or a terror of loneliness, and insensibly welded into a whole, an embryo community. It was a matter of chance, too, in the beginning whether the meeting with another little wandering group would result in bloodshed for the possession of food—sometimes for the possession of women—or a welcome and the joining up of forces; but to the joining-up process there was always a limit—the limit of resources available. A tribe which desired to augment its strength as against its rivals was faced with the difficulty of filling many hungry mouths. . . . Their own community had once been faced with such a difficulty and had solved it by driving out three or four of its weaker members.

"What became of them?" asked Theodore, and was told no one knew. It was winter when food ran short and they were driven out—and some of them had come back after nightfall to the edge of the camp and cried to be allowed in again. Till the men ran out and drove them off with sticks and stone-throwing. After that they went and were no more seen. . . . Later, in the summer, there had broken out a sickness which again reduced their numbers. When the wind blew for long up the valley it brought a bad smell with it—and flies. That was what caused the sickness. There had been a great deal of it; it was said that in a village lower down the river more than half the inhabitants had died.

He surmised as he listened—and realized later—that it was the need of avoiding constant strife that had broken the nomadic habit and solidified the wandering and fluid groups into tribes with a settled dwelling-place. Until a limit was set to their wanderings, groups and single nomads drifted hither and thither in the search for food, snarling at each other when they met; the end of sheer anarchy came with appropriation, by a particular group, of a stretch of country which gave some promise of supporting it. That entailed the institution of communal property, the setting up of a barrier against the incursions of others—a barrier which was also a limit beyond which the group must not trespass on the land and possessions of others. . . . Swiftly, insensibly and naturally, there was growing up a system of boundaries; boundaries established, in the first place, by chance, by force or rough custom and defined later by meetings between headmen of villages. Within its boundaries each tribe or group existed as best it might, overstepping its limits at its peril; but disputing at intervals—as men have disputed since the world began—the precise terms of the agreement that defined its limits. And, agreements being verbal only, there were many occasions for dispute.

As he questioned his new-made comrades and heard their answers, there died in Theodore's heart the hope that these people into whose midst he had stumbled—these people living like the beasts of the field—were but dwellers on the outskirts of a world reviving and civilized. Of men existing in any other fashion than their own he heard no mention, no rumour; there was talk only of a camp here and a village there—where men fished and hunted and scratched the ground that they might find the remains of other's sowing. The formal intercourse between the various groups was suspicious and slyly diplomatic, an affair of the meetings of headmen; though now and again, as life grew more certain, there was trading in the form of barter. One community had settled in a stretch of potato-fields, left derelict, which, even under rough and unskilled cultivation, yielded more than sufficient for its needs; another, by some miracle, had possessed itself of goats—three or four in the first instance, found wild among the hills, escaped from the hungry, indiscriminate slaughter which had bared the countryside of cattle. These they bred, were envied for, guarded with arms in their hands and occasionally bartered; not without bitter resentment and dispute at the price their advantage exacted. . . . But of those who possessed more than goats or the leavings of other men's fields, who lived as men had been wont to live in the days when the world was civilized—not a trace, not so much as a word!

Direct questioning brought only a shake of the head. Towns—yes, of course there were towns—further on; but no one lived in them—you could not get a living out of pavements, bricks and hard roads. . . . Up the river—the way he had come—was a stretch of dead land where nothing grew and no one lived; he had seen it for himself and knew best what lay beyond it. Lower down the river were the other camps like their own; so many they knew of, and others they had heard of further off. In the distance—on the other side of those hills—there had been a large town in the old days; ruins of it—miles of streets and ruins—were lying on both banks of the river. They themselves had never entered it—only seen it from a distance—but those who lived nearer had said it was mostly in ruins and that bodies were thick in the streets. In the summer, they had heard, it was forbidden to enter it; because it was those who had gone there in search of plunder who first were smitten with the sickness which spread from their camp along the valley. It was the wind blowing over the town—so they said—which brought the bad smell and the flies. . . . No, they did not know its name; had never heard it.

It was when he turned from the present to the past that Theodore found himself against a barrier, the barrier unexpected of a plain unwillingness to talk of the world that had vanished. When spoken of at all it was spoken of carefully, with precaution and choosing of phrase, and no man gave easily many details of his life before the Ruin.

At first the strange attitude puzzled him—he could make nothing of the odd, suspicious glances whereby questioning was met, the attempt to parry it, the cautious, non-committal replies; it was only by degrees that he grasped their significance and understood how complete was that renunciation of the past which these people had imposed upon themselves. Forgetfulness—so Theodore learned in time—was more than a precaution; it had been preached in the new-born world as a religion, accepted as an article of faith. The prophet who had expressed the common need and instinct in terms of religion had in due time made his appearance; a wild-eyed, eloquent scare-crow of a man, aflame with belief in his sacred mission and with loathing for the sins of the world. Coming from no one knew where, he carried his gospel through a land left desolate, proclaiming his creed of salvation through ignorance and crying woe on the yet unrepentant sinners who should seek to preserve the deadly knowledge that had brought God's judgment on the world!

The seed of his doctrine fell on fruitful soil—on brutalized minds in starved bodies; the shaggy, half-naked enthusiast was hailed as a law-giver, saint and saviour, and the harvest of souls was abundant. On every side the faith was embraced with fervour; the bitter experience of the convert confirming the prophet's inspiration. Tribe after tribe reconciled itself to a God who had turned in wrath from His creatures, offended by their upstart pretensions and encroachments on the power of Deity. Tribe after tribe made confession of its sin, grovelling at the feet of a jealous Omnipotence and renouncing the works of the devil and the deadly pride of the intellect; and in tribe after tribe there were hideous little massacres—blood-offerings, sweet and acceptable sacrifice, that should purify mankind from its guilt. Those who were known to have pried into the hidden secrets of Omnipotence were cut off in their wickedness, lest they should corrupt others—were dragged to the feet of the prophet and slaughtered, lest they should defile humanity anew through the pride of the intellect and the power of their devil-sent knowledge. Men known to be learned or suspected of learning; men possessed of no more than mechanical training and skill. . . . There was a story of one whom certain in the tribe would have spared—a doctor of medicine who had comforted many in the past. But the prophet cried out that this uttermost sacrifice, too, was demanded of them till, frenzied with piety, they turned on their healer and beat out the brains that had served them. . . . And over the bodies had followed an orgy of repentance, of groaning and revivalistic prayer; the priest blessing the sacrifice with uplifted arms and calling down the vengeance of God Most High upon those who should be false to the vow they had sworn in the blood of sinners. He chanted the vow, they repeating it after him; taking oath to renounce the evil thing, to stamp it out wherever met with, in man, in woman, in child.

The prophet (so Theodore learned) had continued his wanderings, preaching the gospel as he went—through village after village and settlement after settlement, till he passed beyond the confines of report. He had bidden his followers expect his return; but whether he came again or not, his doctrine was firmly established. He had left behind him the germs of a priesthood, a tradition and a Law for his converts—a Law which included the penalty of death for those who should fail to keep the vow. . . .

Lest it should fade from their minds, there were days set apart for renewal of the vow, for public, ceremonial repetition of the creed and doctrine of ignorance; and, with the Ruin an ever-present memory to the remnant of humanity, the tendency was to interpret the Law with all strictness—there were devotees and fanatics who watched with a mingling of animal fear and religious hate for signs of relapse and backsliding. Denunciation was of all things dreaded; and outspoken regret for a world that had passed had more than once been pretext for denunciation. To dwell in speech on the doings of that world might be interpreted—had been interpreted—as a hankering after the Thing Forbidden, a desire to revive the Accursed. . . . Hence the parrying of questions, the barrier of protective silence which the newcomer broke through with difficulty.

It took more than a day for Theodore to understand his new world and its meaning, to grasp its social system and civil and religious polity; but at the end of one day he knew roughly the conditions in which he was destined to live out the rest of his life.

Not that, in the beginning, he admitted that so he must live; it was long—many years—before he resigned himself to the knowledge that his limits, till death released him, were the narrow limits of his tribe. For years he held secretly—but none the less fast—to the hope of a civilization that must one day reveal itself, advance and overwhelm his barbarians. For years he strained his eyes for the coming of its pioneers, its saviours; it was long—very long—before he gave up his hopes and faced the certainty that, if the world he had known continued to exist, it existed too feebly and too far away to stretch out to himself and his surroundings.

There were times when the longing for it flared and burned in him, and he sought desperately for traces of the world he had known—running hither and thither in search of it. Under pretext of a hunting expedition he would absent himself from the tribe, and trespass—often at the imminent risk of death—on the territory of alien communities; returning, after days, no nearer to his goal and no wiser for his stealthy prowlings. The life of alien communities, the prospect revealed from strange hills, was, to all intents and purposes, the life and outlook of his tribe. . . . He would question the occasional stranger from a distant village, in the hope of at least a word, a rumour—a rumour that might give guidance for further and more hopeful search. But those who came from distant villages spoke only of villages more distant; of other hunting-grounds, of other tribal feuds, of other long stretches of ruin. . . . The world, so far as it came within his ken, was cut to one pattern, the pattern of a cowed and brutalized man, who bent his face to the stubborn ground and forgot the cunning of his fathers.

XIX

The actual and formal ceremony of his acceptance into the little community took place after night had fallen; deferred to that hour in part because, with nightfall, the day's labour ceased and the fishermen and snarers of birds had returned to their dwelling-place—and in part because darkness, lit only by the glow of torches and wood fires, lent an added solemnity to the rite.

Earlier in the day the new tribesman had been summoned to a second interview with the headman. The old man questioned him shrewdly enough as to his road, the nature of his winter food store and the feasibility of transporting it; and it was settled finally that Theodore should depart with the morning accompanied by another from the tribe. The pair could row and tow up the river a flat-bottomed boat which was one of the community's possessions; and as his own camp was only a few hours' tramp from navigable water, he and his companion should be able, with a day or two, to make three or four journeys from camp to riverside and load the boat with as much as it would carry of his hoard. If the weather favoured—if snow held off and storm—they might return within five or six days.

His instructions received, he was dismissed; and bidden, since he would need a hut for himself and his wife, to set about its building at once. A site was allotted him on the edge of the copse that was the centre of the tribal life and he was granted the use of some of the tools that were common property—an axe, a mallet, and a spade. By the time the sun set his dwelling had made some progress; stakes had been driven in to serve as corner-posts, and logs laid from one to the other.

With dusk, by twos and threes, the men had drifted back to the village and the women were busied with the cooking of supper at fires that blazed in the open, so long as the weather was dry, as well as at the mud-built ovens that sheltered a flame from the wind. When they kept their men waiting for the plates and bowls of food there was impatient shouting and now and then a blow. . . . Theodore, as he ate his supper, noted suddenly that though one or two of the women carried babies, the camp contained no child that was older than the crawling stage—no child that survived the Disaster.

The night was rainless, and when the meal was over the men, for the most part, lay or crouched near their fires—some torpid, some talking with their women; but they roused and stood upright when the ceremony began, and the headman, calling for silence, beckoned with a dirty claw to Theodore.

"Here!" said Theodore and went to him. The old man was seated on the trunk of a fallen tree; he waited till the tribesmen, one and all, had ranged themselves on either hand and then signed to Theodore to kneel.

"Give me both your hands," he ordered—and held them between his own. As in days long past—(so Theodore remembered)—the overlord, the suzerain, had taken the hands of his vassal. . . . Did he remember—this latter-day barbarian—the ritual of chivalry, the feudal customs of Capet, Hohenstaufen and Plantagenet? Or was his imitation of their lordly rite unconscious?

"So that you may live and be one of us," the old man began, "you will swear two things—to be true to your fellows and humble and meek towards God. Before God and before all of us you will take your oath; and, if you break it, may you die the death of the wicked and may fire consume you to eternity!"

The words were intoned and not spoken for the first time: the ritual of the ceremony was established, and at definite points and intervals the bystanders broke in with a mutter of approval or warning—already traditional.

"First: you will swear, till death takes you, to be our man against all perils and enemies."

"I will be your man till death takes me," swore Theodore, "against all perils and enemies."

"You are witness," said the headman, looking round, and was answered by a murmur from the listeners. The women did not join in it—they had, it seemed, no right of vote or assent; but they had drawn near, every one of them, and were peering at the ceremony from beyond the shoulders of their men.

"And now," came the order, "you will take the oath to God, to purify your heart and renounce devil's knowledge—for yourself and for those who come after you. Swear it after me, word by holy word—and swear it with your heart as with your lips."

And word by word, and line by line, Theodore repeated the formula that cut him off from the world of his youth and the heritage of all the ages. It was a rhythmical formula, its phrasing often Biblical; instinctively the prophet, when he framed his new ritual, had followed the music of the old. . . . Written pages and the stonework of churches might perish, but the word that was spoken endured. . . .

"I do swear and take oath, before God and before man, that I will walk humbly all my days and put from me the pride of the intellect. Remembering that the meek shall inherit the earth and that the poor in spirit are acceptable in the sight of the Most High. Therefore, I do swear and take oath that I will purify my heart of that which is forbidden, that I will renounce and drive out all memory of the learning which it is not meant for me, who am sinful man, to know. What I know and remember of that which is forbidden shall be dead to me and as if it had never been born. . . . May my hands be struck off before I set them to the making of that which is forbidden; and may blindness smite me if I seek to pry into the hidden mysteries of God. Into the secrets of the earth, into the secrets of the air, the secrets of water or fire. For the Lord our God is a jealous God and the secrets of earth, air, water and fire are sacred to Him Who made them and must not be revealed to sinners. . . . Therefore, I pray that my tongue may rot in my mouth before I speak one word that shall kindle the desire of others for that which must not be revealed.

"I call upon the Lord Most High, Who made heaven and earth and all that in them is, to hear this oath that I have sworn; and, in the day that I am false to it, I call on Him to blast me with His utmost wrath. . . . And I call upon my fellow-men to hear this oath that I have sworn; may they shed my blood without mercy, in the day that I am false to it, by thought, word or deed. In the day that I am false to it may they visit my sin on my head; as I will visit their sin on man, woman or child who, in my sight or in my hearing, shall hanker after that which is forbidden.

"For so only shall we cleanse and purify our hearts; so only shall we live without devil's knowledge and bring up our children without it. That the land may have peace in our days and that the wrath of the Most High may be averted from us.

"So help me God. Amen."

"Amen!" came back in a chorus from the shadowy group on either hand; and when the echo of their voices had died in the night the headman loosed Theodore's hands.

He rose and looked round him on the faces that were near enough to see—searched them in the firelight for regret or a memory of the past . . . and, beyond and behind the ring of stolid expressionless faces and the desert silence, saw Markham toasting the centuries, heard the moving thunder of a multitude and the prayer of the Westminster bells. . . .

Lord—through—this—hour . . .

The old man stretched out a hand in token of comradeship admitted—and Theodore took it mechanically.

XX

With dawn Theodore and a stolid companion, appointed by the headman, set out on their journey to the camp where Ada awaited them. They reached it only after weatherbound delays; as they towed their boat against a current that was almost too strong for their paddling they were overtaken by a blinding snowstorm and escaped from it barely with their lives. They made fast their boat to the stump of a tree and groped through the smother to a shed near the river's edge; and there, for the better part of a day, they sheltered while the storm lasted. When it moderated and they pushed on through the dead village, a thick sheet of snow had obliterated the minor landmarks whereby Theodore had been wont to guide his way. It was close upon sunset on the third day of their journey when they trudged into the hidden valley and the familiar tree-clump came in sight—and dusk was thickening into moonless dark when Ada, hearing voices, ran forward with a scream of welcome. She sobbed and laughed incoherently as she clung round her husband's neck; hysterical, perhaps near insanity, through loneliness and the terror of loneliness.

In the intensity of her relief at the ending of her ordeal she forgot, at first, to be greatly disappointed because the world of Theodore's discovery was a world without a cinema or char-à-banc; with her craving for company, it was sheer delight to know that in a few days more she would be in the midst of some two score human beings, whatever their manner of living. It took time and explanation to make her understand that the desire for char-à-banc and cinema must no longer be openly expressed; she stared uncomprehendingly when Theodore strove to make clear to her the religious, as well as the practical, idea that lay behind the prohibition.

The need for caution was the more urgent since he had learned in the course of the return journey that his appointed companion was a fanatic in the new faith, a penitent who groaned to his offended Deity; savagely pure-hearted in the cult of ignorance and savagely suspicious of the backslider.

The religious temperament was something so far removed from Ada's experience that he found it impossible at a first hearing to convince her of the unknown danger of intolerant and distorted faith. His mention of a religious aspect to their new difficulties brought the vague rejoinder that her mother was a Baptist but her aunt had been married in a Catholic church to an Irishman; and in the end he gave up his attempt at explanation and snapped out an order instead.

"You're to be careful how you talk to them. Until you get to know them, you'd better say nothing about what you used to do in the old times. Nothing at all—do you hear? . . ."

She stared, uncomprehending, but realized the order was an order. What she did understand and tremble at was the lack of provision for her coming ordeal of childbirth, and there was a burst of loud weeping and terrified protest when Theodore admitted, in answer to her questions, that he had found no trace of either hospitals, nurses or doctors. For the time being he soothed her with a hurried promise of seeking them further afield—pushing on to find them (they were sure to be found) when she was settled in comfort and safety with other women to look after her. . . . For the time being, he told himself, the soothing deceit was a necessity; she would understand later—see for herself what was possible—settle down and accept the inevitable.

She was all eagerness to start, but it took two full days before the requisite number of journeys had been made to the river—their stores packed on an improvised sled, dragged heavily across the miles of frozen snow and stowed in the flat-bottomed boat. Then, on the third day, Ada herself made the journey; helped along by the men who, when the ground was smooth enough, set her on the sled and dragged her. In spite of their help she needed many halts for rest, and the distance between camp and river took most of the hours of daylight to accomplish; hence they sheltered for the night in a cottage not far from the river's bank, and with morning dropped downstream in the boat—paddling cautiously as they rounded each bend and always on their guard against the possibility of unfriendly meetings. The long desolation they passed through was a no-man's land; any stray hunter, therefore, might deem himself at liberty to attack whom he saw and seize what he found in their possession. But throughout the short day was neither sight nor sound of man and by sunset the current, running swollen and rapidly, had brought them to their destined landing. . . . After that came the mooring of the boat in the reeds and the hiding, on the bank of the river, of the stores they could not carry; then the long uphill tramp over snow, in the gathering darkness—with Ada shivering, crying from weariness and clinging to her husband's arm. And—at last—the glow of fires, through tree-trunks; with figures moving round them, shaggy men and unkempt women. . . . Their home!

The unkempt women met their fellow not unkindly. They drew her to the fire and rubbed her frozen hands; then, while one brought a bowl of steaming mess, another laid dry moss and heather in the bed-place of her unfinished dwelling. A protesting baby was wakened from its sleep and dandled for her comfort and inspection—its mother giving frank and loud-voiced details concerning the manner of its birth. There was a rough and good-natured attempt to raise her drooping spirits, and Ada, fed and warmed, brightened visibly and responded to the clack of tongues. This, at least, the new world had restored to her—the blessing of loud voices raised in chatter. . . . All the same, on the second night of their new life Theodore, awake in the darkness, heard her sniffing and swallowing her tears.

"What is it?" he asked and she clung to him miserably and wept her forebodings on his shoulder. Not only forebodings of her coming ordeal in the absence of hospitals and doctors, but—was this, in truth, to be the world?

These people—so they told her—knew of no other exist-ing; but what had become of all the towns? The trams, the shops, the life of the towns—her life—where was it? It must be somewhere—a little way off—where was it? . . . He soothed her with difficulty, repeating his warnings on the danger of open regrets for the past and remind-ing her that to-morrow she also would be called on for the oath.

"I know," she whimpered. "Of course I'll taike an oath if I must. But you can't 'elp thinking—if you swear yourself black in the faice, you can't 'elp thinking."

"Whatever you think," he insisted, "you mustn't say it—to anyone."

"I know," she snuffled obediently, "I shan't say noth-ing . . . but, oh Gawd, oh Gawd—aren't we ever going to be 'appy again?"

He knew what she was weeping for—shaking with mis-erable sobs; the evenings at the pictures, the little bits of machine-made finery, the petty products of "devil's knowledge" that had made up her daily life. The cry to her "Gawd" was a prayer for the return of these things and the hope of them had so far sustained her in peril, hardship and loneliness. Pictures and finery had always been there, just a mile or two beyond the horizon—awaiting her enjoyment so soon as it was safe to reach them. Now, in her overpowering misery and darkness of soul, she was facing the dread possibility that they no lon-ger awaited her, that the horizon was immeasurable, infi-nite. . . . Guns and bombs and poisons—nobody wanted them and she understood people making up their minds to do without 'em. But the other things—you couldn't go on living without the other things—shops and proper houses and railways. . . .

"It can't be for always," she persisted, "it can't be"—and was cheered by the sudden heat of his agreement, the sudden note of protest in his voice. The knowledge that he sympathized encouraged her and, with her head on his shoulder, sniffing, but comforted, she began to plan out their deliverance.

"They must be somewhere—the people that live like they used to. Keepin' quiet, I dessay, till things gets more settled. When things is settled they'll get a move on and come along and find us. It stands to reason they can't be so very far off, because I remember the teacher tellin' us when we 'ad our jography lesson that England's quite a small country. So they 'aven't got so very far to come. . . . I expect an aeroplane'll come first."

He felt her thrill in expectation of the moment when she sighted the swiftly moving speck aloft, the bearer of deliverance drawing nigh. Wouldn't it be heavenly when they saw one at last—after all these awful months and years! . . . In the war they were beastly, but, now that the war was over, what had become of all the passenger 'planes and the airships? She was always looking out for one—always; every morning when she came out of the hut the first thing she did was to look up at the sky. . . . And some day one was bound to come. When things had settled down and got straight, it was bound to. . . .

But it never did; and in the end she ceased to look for it.

His attempts—they were many in the first few years—to break away from his world and his bondage of ignorance were made always with cunning precaution and subterfuge; not even the pitiable need of his wife would have served as excuse for the backsliding which was search after the forbidden. To a fanaticism dominated by the masculine element the pains of childbirth were once more an ordinance of God; and when, a few weeks before Ada's time of trial, Theodore absented himself from the camp for a night or two, he gave no one (save Ada) warning of his journey, and later accounted for his absence by a plausible story of straying and a hunter's misfortunes. He had ceased, since he took up his dwelling with the tribe, to believe in the neighbourhood of a civilization in being; all he hoped for was the neighbourhood, not too distant, of men who had not acquiesced in ruin and put hope of recovery behind them. What he sought primarily was that aid and comfort in childbirth for which his wife appealed to him with insistence that grew daily more terrified; what he sought fundamentally was escape from a people vowed to ignorance.

The goal of his first journey was the town lying lower down the river, the forbidden city which had once bred pestilence and flies. He approached it deviously, keeping to the hills and avoiding districts he knew to be inhabited; hoping against hope, that, in spite of report, he might find some rebuilding of a civic existence and human life as he had known it. . . . What he found when he came down from the foothills and trudged through its outskirts was the customary silent desolation; a desolation flooded and smelling of foul water—untenanted streets that were channels and backwaters, and others where the slime of years lay thick and scum bred rank vegetation.

Silent streets and empty houses had long been familiar to him, but until that day he had not known how swiftly nature, left to herself, could take hold of them. The river and the life that sprang from it was overwhelming what man had deserted. Three winters of neglect in a low-lying, well-watered country had wrought havoc with the work of the farmer and the engineer; streams which had been channelled and guided for centuries had already burst their way back to freedom. With every flooded winter more banks were undermined, more channels silted up and shifted; and that which had been ploughland, copse or water-meadow was relapsing into bog undrained. The valley above and below the town was a green swamp studded with reedy little pools; a refuge for the waterbird where a man would set foot at his peril. Buildings here and there stood rotting, forlorn and inaccessible—barns, sheds and farmhouses, their walls leaning drunkenly as foundations shifted in the mud; and in the town itself, as surely, if more slowly, the waters were taking possession. . . . Towns had vanished, he knew—vanished so completely that their very sites had been matter of dispute to antiquarians—but never till to-day had he visualized the process; the rising of layer on layer of mud, the sapping of foundations by water. The forces that made ruin and the forces that buried it; flood and frost and the persistent thrust of vegetation. As the waterlogged ground slid beneath them, rows of jerry-built houses were sagging and cracking to their fall; here and there one had crumbled and lay in a rubble heap, the water curdling at its base. . . . How many life-times, he wondered, till the river had the best of it and the houses where men had gone out and in were one and all of them a rubble heap—under water and mud and rank greenery? He saw them, decades or centuries ahead, as a waste, a stretch of bogland where the river idled; bogland, now flooded, now drying and cracked in the sun; and with broken green islets still thrusting through the swamp—broken green islets of moss-covered rock that underneath was brick and mortar. In time it might be—with more decades or centuries—the islets also would sink lower in the swamp, disappear. . . .

The process, unhindered, was certain as sunrise; the important little streets that humanity had built for its vanished needs and its vanished business would be absorbed into an indifferent wilderness, in all things sufficient to itself. The rigid important little streets had been no more than an episode in the ceaseless life of the wilderness; an episode ending in failure, to be decently buried and forgotten.

He plodded aimlessly through street after street that was fordable till the shell of a "County Infirmary" mocked at Ada's hopes and recalled the first purpose of his journey; a gaunt sodden building, the name yet visible on walls that sweated fungi and mould. Then, that he might leave nothing undone in the way of help and search, he trudged and waded to the lower outskirts of the town; where the roads lost themselves in grass and flooded water, and there stretched to the limit of his eyesight a dull winter landscape without sign of living care or habitation. In the end—having strained his eyes after that which was not—he turned to slink back to his own place; skirting alien territory where the sight of a stranger might mean an alarm and a manhunt, and sheltering at night where his fire might be hidden from the watcher.

"You 'aven't found nothin'?" Ada whimpered, when he had told his necessary lies to the curious and they were out of earshot in their hut. Her eyes had grown piteous when he stumbled in alone; she had dreamt in his absence of sudden and miraculous deliverance—following him in fancy through streets with tramlines, where dwelt women who wore corsets—also doctors. Who, perhaps, when they knew the greatness of her need, would send a motor-ambulance—to fetch her to a bed with sheets on it.

"Nothing," he told her almost roughly, afraid to show pity. "No doctors, no houses fit to live in. Wherever I've been and as far as I could see—it's like this."

XXI

It was in the third spring after the Ruin of Man that Ada's time was accomplished and she bore a son to her husband; on a day in late April or early May there was going and coming round the shelter that was Theodore's home. The elder women of the tribe, by right of their experience, took possession, and from early morning till long after nightfall they busied themselves with the torment and mystery of birth; and with the aid of nothing but their rough and unskilled kindliness Ada suffered and brought forth a squalling red mannikin—the heir of the ages and their outcast. The child lived and, despite its mother's fecklessness, was lusty; as a boy, ran shoeless, and, in summer, naked as Adam; and grew to his primitive manhood without letters, knowing of the world that was past and gone only legends derived from his elders.

His coming, to Theodore, meant more than paternity; the birth of his son made him one with the life of the tribe. By the child's wants and helplessness—still more when other children followed—his father was tied to an existence which offered the necessary measure of security; to the stretch of land where he had the right to hunt unmolested, the patch he had the right to sow and reap, and the company of those who would aid him in protecting his children. He had given his hostages to fortune and the limits set to his secret expeditions in search of a lost world were the limits set by the needs of those dependent on him, by his fear of leaving them too long unprotected, unprovided for.

He learned much from his firstborn and the brothers and sisters who followed him; not only the intimate lore of his fatherhood, but the lore and outlook of man bred uncivilized, and the traditions, in making, of a world to come—which in all things would resemble the old traditions handed down by a world that had died. His children lived naturally the life that had been forced upon their father and inherited ignorance as a birthright; growing up—such as lived through the perils of childhood—without knowledge of the past and untempted by the sin of the intellect. The oath which Theodore, like every new-made father, was called on to swear in the name of the child he had given to the tribe, had a meaning to those who had lived through Disaster and witnessed the Ruin of Man; to the next generation the vow was a formula only, a renunciation of that they had never possessed. They could not, if they would, instruct their children in the secrets of God, the forbidden lore of the intellect.

By the time his first son was of an age to think and question, Theodore understood more than the growth and workings of a child-mind—much that had hitherto seemed dark and fantastic in the origins of a world that had ended with the Ruin of Man. It was the workings of a child-mind that made oddly clear to him the signifi-cance of primitive religious doctrine and beliefs handed down through the ages—the once meaningless doctrine of the Fall of Man and the belief in a vanished Golden Age. These the boy, unprompted, evolved from his own knowledge and the talk of his elders, accepting them spontaneously and naturally.

In Theodore's childhood the Golden Age had been a myth and pleasant fancy of the ancients, and the Fall of Man as distant as the Book of Genesis and unreal as the tale of Puss-in-Boots; to his children, one and all, the legends of his infancy were close and undoubted realities. The Golden Age was a wondrous condition of yesterday; the Fall—the Ruin—its catastrophic overthrow, an experience their father had survived. The fields and hillsides where they worked, played and wandered were still littered with strange relics of the Golden Age—the vanished, fruitful, incomprehensible world whence their parents had been cast into the outer darkness of everyday hardship as a penalty for the sin of mankind. The sin unforgivable of grasping at the knowledge which had made them like unto gods; a mad ambition which not only they but their children's children must atone for in the sweat of their brow. . . . More than once Theodore suspected in the secret recesses of his youngsters' minds a natural and wondering contempt for the men of the last generation; the fools and blind who had overreached themselves and forfeited the splendour of the Golden Age by their blundering greed and unwisdom. So history was writing itself in their minds; making of a race that had acquiesced in science and drifted to destruction a legendary people whose sin was deliberate—a people whose encroachments had angered a self-important Deity and brought

down his wrath upon their heads. It was a history insepa-
rable from religious belief; its opening chapters identical
in all essentials with the legendary history of an epoch
that had ceased to exist.

Once his eight-year boy, planted sturdily before him,
demanded a plain explanation of the folly of his father's
contemporaries.

"Why," he asked frowning, "did the people want to find
out God's secrets?"

Theodore thought of Ada and the countless millions
like her, leaned his chin on his hand and smiled grimly.

"Some of us didn't," he answered. "Some of us—many
of us—had no interest in the secrets of God. We made use
of them when others found them out, but we, ourselves,
were quite content to be ignorant. Ignorant in all things."

"I know," the child assented, puzzled by his father's
smile. "The good ones didn't want to—the good ones like
you and Mummy. But the others—all the wicked ones—
why did they? It was stupid of them."

"They wanted to find out," said Theodore, "and there
have always been people like that. From the beginning,
the very beginning of things—ever since there were men
on the earth. The desire to know burned them like a fire.
There is an old story of a woman who brought great trouble into the world because she wanted to know. She was
given a box and told never to open it; but she disobeyed
because she was filled with a great curiosity to know what
had been put inside it. Her longing tormented her night
and day and she could think of nothing else; till at last
she opened the box and horrible creatures flew out."

The boy, interested, demanded more of Pandora and the horrible creatures. "Is it a true story?" he asked when his father had given such further details as he managed to remember and invent.

"Yes," Theodore told him, "I believe it is a true story. It was so long ago that we cannot tell exactly how it happened: I may not have told it you quite rightly, but on the whole it is a true story. . . . And the wicked people—our wicked people who brought ruin on the world—were much like Pandora and her box. It was the same thing over again; they wanted to know so strongly that they forgot everything else; they had only the longing to find out and it seemed as if nothing else mattered."

"Weren't they afraid?" the boy asked doubtfully, still puzzled by his father's odd smile. "Afraid of what would happen to them?"

"No," Theodore answered. "Until it was too late and they saw what they had done, I don't think many were afraid. Here and there, before the end, some began to be frightened, but most of them didn't see where they were going."

"But they must have known," his son insisted, frowning. "God told them He would punish them if they tried to learn His secrets."

"Yes," Theodore assented—with the orthodox truth, more deceptive than a lie, that meant one thing to him and another to the world barbarian. "Yes, God told them so; but though He said it very plainly not many of them understood. . . ." They were talking, he knew, across more than the gulf between the mind of a child and a man; between them lay the centuries, the barrier of many generations. To his son, now and always, dead and gone chemists and mathematicians must appear in the likeness of present evildoers—raiders of the territory and robbers of the property of God; to his son, now and always, inventors and spectacled professors in mortarboards would be greedy, foolish chieftains who planned war against Heaven as a tribe plans assault upon its rivals. These were and must always be his "wicked," his destroyers of the Golden Age; his life and outlook being what it was, how should he picture the war against Heaven as pure-hearted, instinctive and unconscious?

"Why not?" the child persisted, repeating the question when his father stroked his head absently.

"Because . . . they did not know themselves. If they had known themselves and their own passions they would have seen why knowledge was forbidden."

"Yes," said the child vaguely—and passed to the matter that interested him.

"Why didn't the others make them understand? You and the other good ones?"

"Because," said Theodore, "we ourselves didn't understand. That was the blunder—the sin—of the rest of us. We didn't seek after knowledge, but we took the fruits of other men's knowledge and ate."

(Unconsciously he made use of the familiar hereditary simile.)

"I'd have killed them," his son declared firmly. "Every one. I'd have told them to stop, and then, if they wouldn't, I'd have killed them. Thrown them in the river—or hammered them with stones till they died. That's what I'd have done."

"No," Theodore told him, "you wouldn't have killed them. . . . One of them said the same thing to me—one of the wicked ones. He said we should have stamped out the race of them. Afterwards I knew he was right, but at the time I didn't understand. I couldn't. I heard what he said, but the words had no real meaning for me."

He saw something that was almost contempt in his son's eyes and took the grubby face between his hands.

"That same wicked man—who was also very wise—told me something else that is as true for you as it was for me; he said that we never know anything except through our own experience. I might tell you that the sun is warm or the water is cold, but if you had never felt the heat of the sun or the cold of the water you would not know what I meant. And it was like that with us; there were always some few who understood that knowledge was a flame that, in the end, would burn us—but the rest of us couldn't even try to save ourselves until after we were burned."

He stroked the grubby face as he released it.

"That's the Law, son; and all that matters you'll learn that way. That way and no other—just as we did."

In time he found himself recalling, with strange interest, the fairy-tales of his childhood; he spent long hours re-weaving and piecing them together, searching his memory for half-remembered fragments of what had once seemed fantasy or nonsense invented for the nursery. The hobgoblins and heroes of his nursery days were transformed and made suddenly possible; looking through the mind of a new generation, he saw that they might have been as human and prosaic as himself. More—he came to know that he and his commonplace, civilized contemporaries would be the heroes and hobgoblins of the future.

The process, the odd transformation, would be simple as it was inevitable. It was forbidden, by the spirit and letter of the Vow, to awaken youthful curiosity concerning the past—youthful curiosity whose end might be youthful experiment; but women, in spite of all vows and prohibitions, would gossip to each other of their memories. While they talked their children would listen, open-eyed and puzzled; and when a youngster demanded the meaning of an unfamiliar term or impossible happening, the explanation, as a matter of course, took the form of analogy, of comparison with the known and familiar. The aeroplane was a bird extinct and monstrous—larger, many times larger, than the flapping heron or the owl; the bomb was more dreadful than a lightning stroke; the tram, train or motor a gigantic wheelbarrow that ran without man or beast to drag it. . . . The ignorance of science of those who told, the yet greater ignorance of those who heard, resulted, inevitably, before many years had passed, in myth and religious legend—an outwardly fantastic statement of actual fact and truth. The children, piecing together their fragments of incomprehensible information, made their own image of the past—to be handed on later to their sons; an image of a world fantastic, enchanted and amazing, destroyed, as a judgment for sin against God, by strange, fire-breathing beasts and bolts from heaven. A world of gigantic fauna and bewitched chariots; likewise of sorcerers, their masters—whom God and the righteous had exterminated. . . . So Theodore realized—as his children grew and he heard them talk—must a race that knew nothing of science explain the dead wonders of science; from the message that flashes round the world in seconds to the petrol-engine and the magic slumber of chloroform. That which is outside the power and beyond the understanding of man has always been denounced as magic; and steam, electricity, chemical action, were outside the power and beyond the understanding of men born after the Ruin. In default of understanding they must needs fall back on a wizardry known to their fathers; thus he and his contemporaries to their children's children would be semi-supernatural beings, fit comrades of Sindbad, of Perseus, or the Quatre Fils Aymon: giants with great voices that called to each other across continents and vasty deeps; possessors of seven-league boots, magic steeds and flying carpets—of all the stock-in-trade of the fairy-tale. . . . Belief in the demi-god was a natural growth and product of the world wherein his son grew to manhood.

Given time and black ignorance of mechanics and science, and the engineer would be promoted to a giant or demi-god; who, by virtue of a strength that was more than human, dammed rivers, drained bogs and pierced mountains. "As it was in the beginning, is now and ever shall be"—and always in the past there had been giants.

Titans—and Hercules, removing mighty obstacles and cleansing the stables of Augeas. He came to understand that all wonders were facts misinterpreted and that (given time and ignorance) a post-office underling, tapping out his Morse code, might be seen as a geni or an Oberon—the absolute master of obedient sprites who could lay their girdles round the earth; and he pictured a college-bred, sober-suited Hercules planning his Labours in the office of a limited company—jotting down figures, estimating costs and scanning the reports of geologists. Figures and reports, like his tunnels and dams, would pass into the limbo of science forgotten and forbidden, but the memory of his labours, his defiance of brute nature, would live on as the story of a demi-god; and the childhood that was barbarism would explain his achievements by a giant strength that could tear down trees and move mountains.

The idea took fast root and grew in him—the idea of a world that, time and again, had returned to the help-lessness of childhood. He saw science as the burden that, time and again, the race found intolerable; as Dead-Sea fruit that turned to ashes in the mouth, as riches that humanity strove for, attained and renounced—renounced because it dared not keep them. In his hours of dreaming he made fairies and demi-gods out of dapper little sedentary persons, the senders of forgotten telegrams, with forgotten engines—motor-cars and aeroplanes—at their insignificant command; and once, in the night, when Ada snored beside him, he asked himself if Lucifer, Son of the Morning—Lucifer who strove with his God and was worsted—were more, in his beginnings, than a scientist intent on his work? A chemist, a spectacled professor, resplendent only in degrees and learning? An Archfiend of Knowledge who had sinned against God in the secret places of a laboratory and not upon the shining plains of Heaven? And whom ignorance and time had glorified into the Tempter, the Evil One—setting him magnificently in the flaming Hell which he and his like, by their skill and patience, had created and let loose upon man? . . . This, at least, was certain; that in years to come and under other names, his children's children would retell the story of Lucifer, Son of the Morning; the Enemy of Man who was flung out of Heaven because, in his overweening vanity, he encroached on the power of a God.

It was the new world that taught him that man invents nothing, is incapable of pure invention; that what seem his wildest, most fantastic imaginings are no more than ineffective, distorted attempts to set down a half-forgotten experience. What had once appeared prophecies he saw to be memories; the Day of Judgment, when the heavens should flame and men call upon the rocks to cover them, belonged to the past before it belonged to the future. The forecast of its terrors was possible only to a people that had known them as realities; a people troubled by a dim race-memory of the conquest of the air and catastrophe hurled from the skies. . . .

So, at least, his children taught him to believe.

XXII

With years and rough husbandry the resources of the tribe were augmented and it emerged from its first starved misery; more land was brought under cultivation and, as tillage improved and better crops were raised, the little community was less dependent on the haphazard luck of its fishing and snaring and lived further from the line of utter want. While, save in bad seasons, the inter-tribal raiding that was caused by sheer starvation was less frequent. Even so, strife was frequent enough—small intermittent feud that flared now and again into savagery; the desire of a growing community to extend its hunting-grounds at the expense of a neighbour meant, almost inevitably, appeal to the right of the strongest. Other quarrels had their origin in the border inroads and repri-sals of poachers or a barbaric setting of the eternal story that was old when Helen launched a thousand ships.

With husbandry, even rough husbandry, came the small beginnings of commerce, the barter and exchange of one man's superfluities for the produce of another man's fields. Cold and nakedness stimulated ingenuity in the matter of clothing, even in a society whose origi-nal members had in large part been bred to depend in all things on the aid of the machine and to earn a liveli-hood by the performance of one action only—the tending of one lathe, the accomplishment of one stereotyped mechanical process. Outcasts of civilization flung into the world of savagery, they had in the beginning none of the adaptability and none of the resources of the savage— knew nothing of the properties of unfamiliar plants, knew neither what to weave nor how to weave it, and often from sheer lack of understanding, starved and shivered in the midst of plenty. It was not till they had suffered long and intolerably that they learned to clothe themselves from such material as their new world afforded, to cure skins of animals and stitch them together into garments. In the first years of ruin only ratskins were plentiful; but, as time went on, rabbits, cats and wild dogs multiplied and, spreading through the countryside, were trapped and hunted for their flesh and the warmth of their skins. The dogs, as they bred, reverted to a mongrel and wolf-like type which, in summer, preyed largely on vermin; in winter, when scarcity of food made them bold, they prowled in packs, were a danger to the solitary and a legendary terror to children.

In the beginning the village was a straggle of rude huts, the tribesmen building how and where they would; later it took shape within its first wall and was roughly circular, enclosed by a fence of stake and thornbush. The raising of the fence was a sign and result of the beginning of primitive competition in armament; it was the knowledge that one village had fortified itself that set others to the driving in of stakes. One November evening Theodore, trudging in with his catch, saw a group round the headman's fire; the centre of interest, a youth who had returned from poaching on other men's land and brought back news of their doings. His trespassing had taken him within sight of the neighbouring village—which lately was a cluster of huts, like their own, and now was surrounded by a wall. A stockade, fully the height of a man, with only one gap for a gate. . . . The poacher's news was discussed with uneasy interest. The fortified tribe, in point of numbers, was already stronger than its rival; if it added this new advantage to its numbers, what was there to prevent it from raiding and robbing as it would? Having raided and robbed, it could shelter behind its defences—beat off attack, make sorties and master the countryside! Its security meant the insecurity of others, the dependence of others on its goodwill and neighbourly honesty; the issue was as plain to the handful of tribesmen as to old-time nations competing in battleships, aeroplanes and guns, and the suspicions muttered round the headman's fire were the raw material of arguments once familiar in the councils of emperors.

In the end, as the result of uneasy discussion, Theodore and another were dispatched to spy out the new menace, to get as near as they might to the wall, ascertain its strength and the method of its building; and with their return from a night expedition there was more consultation and a hurried planning of defences. Before winter was over the haphazard settlement was a compound, a walled town in embryo; within the narrow limits of a circle small enough for a handful of men to defend all huts were crowded, all provisions stored, all animals driven at sunset—so that, in case of night attack, no man could be cut off and the strength of the tribe be at hand to resist the assailants. With waste, healthy miles stretching out on either side, the village itself was an evil-smelling huddle of cabins; since a short stretch of wall was easier to defend than a long, men and beasts were crowded together in a foulness that made for security. In times of feud—and times of feud were seldom distant—stones were heaped beside the barrier, in readiness to serve as missiles, watch and ward was kept turn and turn by the able-bodied and—naturally, inevitably and almost unconsciously—there was evolved a system of military discipline, of penalty for mutiny and cowardice.

As in every social system from the beginning of time, the community was welded to a conscious whole not by the love its members bore to each other, but by hatred and fear of the outsider; it was the enemy, the urgent common need to be saved from him, that made of man a comrade and a citizen; the peril from outside was the natural antidote to everyday hatreds and the ceaseless bickerings of close neighbours. The instinctive politics of a squalid village were in miniature the policy of vanished nations, and untraditioned little headmen, like dead and gone kings, quelled internal feuds by diverting attention to the danger that threatened from abroad. The foundations of community life in the new world, like the foundations of community life in the old, were laid in the selfishness of fear; but for all its base origin the life of the community imposed upon its members the essential virtues of the soldier and citizen, a measure of discipline and sacrifice. From these, in time, would grow loyalty and pride in sacrifice; the enclosure of ramshackle huts and pens was breaking its savages to achievements undreamed of and virtues as yet beyond their ken; the blind, stubborn instincts that created Babylon—created London and Rome and destroyed them—were laying well and truly in a mud-walled compound the foundations of cities which should rise, flourish, perish in the stead of London and of Rome.

Outside the little fortress with its noisome huddle of sheds and shelters lay a belt of ploughed land, of patches scraped and sown, where the women worked by the side of their men and worked alone when their men were gone hunting or fishing. One or two members of the tribe who were countrymen born were its saviours in its first years of leanness, imparting their knowledge of soil and seed to their unskilled comrades bred in towns; and, by slow degrees, as the lesson was learned, the belt of tilled ground grew wider and more fertile, the little community more prosperous.

As families grew and the tribe settled down the make-shift shelters of wood and moss were succeeded by stronger and better built cabins; by the time that her second child was born Ada was established in a weatherproof hut—a mud-walled building, roofed with dried grass and with a floor of earth beaten hard. In its early years it possessed a glazed window, a pane which Theodore had found whole in a crumbling house and set immovably in an aperture cut in his wall. But, as years went on, unbroken glass was hard to come by; and there came a day when the window-aperture, no longer glazed, was plastered up to keep out the weather.

Long before he set about the building of his cabin Theodore had brought a strip of ground under cultivation, sown a patch of potatoes and straggling beans which, in time, expanded to a field. His life, henceforth, was largely the anxious life of the seasons; the sowing and tending and reaping of his crop, the struggle with the soil and the barrenness thereof, the ceaseless war against vermin. . . . He ended rich, as the men of his time counted riches; the possessor of goats, the owner of land which other men envied him, the father of sons who could till it. The new world gave him what it had to give; and gradually, with the passing of years, the hope of life civilized died in him and he ceased to strain his eyes at the distance.

It was slowly, very slowly, that hope died in him; but there came a day when, searching the skyline, as his habit was, it dawned on his mind that he sought automatically; it was habit only that made him lift his eyes to the horizon. He expected nothing when he shaded his eyes and looked this way and that; his belief in a world that was lettered and civilized had vanished. If that world yet existed, remote and apart, of a surety it was not for him—who perhaps was no longer capable of existence lettered and civilized. And if he himself could be broken to its decencies, what place had his children, his young barbarians, in an ordered atmosphere like that of his impossible youth?

They belonged to their world, to its squalor, its dirt, its rude ignorance . . . as, it might be, he also belonged.

At the thought, he knelt and stared into the water, taking stock of the image it reflected and coming face to face with himself. His body and habits had adapted themselves to their surroundings, his mind to the outlook of his world—to his daily, yearly struggle with the soil and vermin and his fellows. His relations with his fellows—with women—with himself—were not those of humanity civilized; it was nothing to him to go foul and unwashed or to clench his fist against his wife. Could he live the life he had been born and bred to, of cleanliness, self-control and courtesy? Or had he been stripped of the decencies which go to make civilized man? . . . He covered his face with his broken-nailed fingers and strove with God and his own soul that he might not fall utterly to ruin with his world, that some remnant might remain of his heritage.

From the day when he saw himself for what he was and resigned all hope of the world of his youth, it seemed to him that he lived two divergent lives. One absorbed, perforce, in his digging and snaring, in the daily struggle, for the daily wants of his household; the other—in his hours of summer rest, in the long dark winter evenings—an inward life of brooding that concerned itself only with the past. His memories became to him a species of cult, a secret ceremonial and a rite; that which had been (so he fancied) was not altogether waste, not altogether dead, so long as one man thought of it with reverence. When the mood took him he would sit for long hours with his chin on his hand, staring at the fire while the children wondered at his silence—and Ada, wearied of talking to deaf ears, flung off to gossip with the neighbours.

She, before she was thirty, was a haggard slattern of a woman; pitiable by reason of her discontent, and looking far older than her years. Childbearing aged her and the field-work she hated—the bent-backed drudgery she tried in vain to shirk and to which she brought no shred of understanding; even more she was aged by the weary desire that sulked in the corners of her mouth. Before she lost her comeliness she had more than once sought distraction from her dullness in clumsy flirtation; which perhaps was no more than silly ogling and nudging and perhaps led to actual unfaithfulness. Theodore—not greatly interested in his wife's doings—ignored the danger to his household peace until it was forcibly thrust upon his notice by a jealous spitfire who cursed Ada for running after other women's husbands, and proceeded to tear out her hair. Ada's snuffling protestations when the spitfire was pulled off did not savour of injured innocence; he judged her guilty, at least in thought, cuffed her soundly and from that time kept his eye on her. He was not (as she liked to think) jealous—salving her bruises with the comforting balm that two males were disputing the possession of her body; what stirred him to wrath fundamentally was his outraged sense of property in Ada, his woman, and the possibility that her lightness might entail on him the labour of supporting another man's child. The intrigue—if intrigue it were—ended on the day of the cuffing and hairpulling; her Lothario, awed by

Theodore Savage

his spitfire or unwilling to tackle an outraged husband, avoided her company from that day forth and Ada sank back to domesticity.

She, too, in the end accepted the loss of the world that had made her what she was, ceased to search the horizon and strain her eyes for the deliverer; whereupon—having nothing to aim at or hope for—she lapsed into slovenly neglect of her home, alternating hours of clack and gossip with fits of sullen complaining at the daily misery of existence.

Had destiny realized the dreams of her youth and set her to live out her married life in a shoddy little villa with bamboo furniture, she might have made a tolerable mother; she would at least have taken pride in the looks of her children, have dressed them with interest, as she dressed herself, and tied up their hair with satin bows. Being what she was, she could take no pride in ragamuffins who ran half the year naked; she could see no beauty, even, in straight agile limbs which were meant to be encased in reach-me-down suits or cheap costumes of cotton velveteen. Thus her naked little ragamuffins— those of them that lived—were apt to be dirtier, less cared-for, than the run of the dirty village youngsters. Theodore, in whom the instinct of fatherhood was strong, was sometimes roused to wrath by her stupid mishandling of her children; but, on the whole he was patient with her— knowing it useless to be otherwise. He beat her as seldom as possible and she was looked on by her neighbours as a woman kindly handled and unduly blessed in her husband. To the end she remained what she had always been; essentially a parasite, a minor product of civilization, machine-bred and crowd-developed—bewildered by a life not lived in crowds and not subject to the laws of the Machine. To the end all nature was alien and hateful to her—raw life that she turned from with disgust. . . . In her last illness her mind, when it wandered, strayed back into the world where she belonged; Theodore, an hour before she died, heard her muttering of "last Bank 'Oliday."

She died at the end of a long hard winter during which she had failed and complained unceasingly, sat huddled to the fire and grown weaker; creeping, at last, to her straw in the corner and forgetting, in delirium, the meaningless life she had shared with her husband and children. Death smoothed out the lines in her sullen face; it was peaceful, almost comely, when Theodore looked his last on it—and wondered, oddly, if among the "many mansions," were some Cockney paradise of noise and jostle where his wife had found her heart's desire?

Of the four or five children she had brought into the world but two were living on the day of her death, her eldest-born and a youngster at the crawling stage; but the care of even two children was a burdensome matter for a man unaided, and it was esteemed natural and no insult to the dead, that Theodore should take another wife as speedily as might be—in the course not of months but of weeks. He found a woman to suit his needs without going further than his own tribe; a woman left widowed a year or two before, who was glad enough to accept the offer of a better living than she could hope to make by her own scratching of a rod or two of earth and the uncertain charity of neighbours. The proposal of marriage, made in stolid fashion, was accepted as a matter of course . . . and, that night, Theodore stared through the fire into a room in Westminster where a girl in a yellow dress made music . . . and a young man listened from the corner of a sofa with a cigarette, unlit, between his fingers. He was dreaming at a table—with silver and branching yellow roses—when his son nudged him that supper was ready, and he dipped his hand into a greasy bowl for the meat.

The wedding followed swiftly on the heels of betrothal, and was celebrated in the manner already compulsory and established; by a public promise made solemnly before the headman, by a clasping of hands and a ceremony of religious blessing. This last was moulded, like all tribal ceremonies, on remembered formulæ and ritual; and the tradition that a wedding should be accompanied by much eating and general merrymaking was also faithfully observed.

The new wife, if not over comely or intelligent, was a sturdy young woman who had been broken to the duties required of her, and Theodore's home, under its second mistress, was better tended and more comfortable than in the days of her sluttish predecessor. He had married her simply as a matter of business, that she might help in his field-work, cook his food, look after his children and satisfy his animal desire; and on the whole he had no reason to complain of the bargain he had made. She was a younger woman than Ada by some years—had been only a slip of a girl at the time of the Ruin—and, because of her youth, had adapted herself more readily than most of her elders to a world in the making and untraditioned methods of living. Her husband found life easier for the help of a pair of sturdy arms and pleasanter for lack of Ada's grumbling. . . . She brought more than herself to Theodore's household—a child by her first husband; and, as time went on, she bore him other children of his own.

XXIII

As the years went by and his children grew to manhood in the world primitive which was the only world they knew, the life of Theodore Savage became definitely twofold; a life of the body in the present and a life of the mind in the past. There was his outward, rustic and daily self, the labourer, hunter and fisherman, who begat sons and daughters, who trudged home at nightfall to eat and sleep heavily, who occasionally cudgelled his wife: a sweating, muscular animal man whose existence was bounded by his bodily needs and the bodily needs of his children; who fondled his children and cuffed them by turns, as the beast cuffs and fondles its offspring. Whose world was the world of a food-patch enclosed in a valley, of a river where he fished, a wood where he snared and a hut that received him at evening. . . . In time it was of these things, and these things only, that he spoke to his kin and his neighbours; the weather, the luck of his hunting or fishing, the loves, births and deaths of his fellows. With the rise and growth of a generation that knew only the world primitive, the little community lived more in the present and less in the past; mention of the world that had vanished was even less frequent and even more furtive than before.

And even if that had not been the case, there was no man in the tribe, save Theodore, whose mind was the mind of a student; thus his other life, his life of the past, was lived to himself alone. It was a vivid memory-life in which he delved, turning over its vanished treasures— the intangible treasures of dead beauty, dead literature, learning and art; a life that at times receded to a dream of the impossible and at others was so real and overwhelming in its nearness that the everyday sweating and toiling and lusting grew vague and misty—was a veil drawn over reality.

Sometimes the two lives clashed suddenly and oddly— to the wonder of those who saw him. As on the day when his wife had burned the evening mess and, raising his hand to chastise her carelessness, there flashed before his eyes, without warning, a vision of Phillida bent delicately over her piano. . . . Not only Phillida, but the room, her surroundings; every detail clear to him and the loveliness of Chopin in his ears. . . . Furniture, hangings, a Louis Seize clock and a Hogarth print—and swiftly-seen objects whose very names he had forgotten, so long was it since he had made use of the household words that once described them. The dead world caught him back to itself and claimed him; in the face of its reality the present faded, the burned stew mattered not and his hand dropped slack to his side; while his wife's mouth, open for a wailing protest, hung open in gratified astonishment. He stared through the open door of the hut, not seeing the tufted trees beyond it or the curving skyline of the hills; then, taking mechanically his stout wooden spoon, he shovelled down his portion without tasting it. In his ears, like a song, was the varied speech of other days; of art, of daily mechanics, of books, of daily politics, of learning. . . . Phillida, her curved hands touching the keys, gave place to the eager, bespectacled face of a scholar who had tried to make clear to him the rhythm and beauty of French verse. He had forgotten the man's name—long forgotten it—but from some odd crevice in his brain a voice came echoing down the years, caressing the lines as it quoted them:—

> O Corse à cheveux plats, que la France était belle
> Au soleil de Messidor!

His own lips framed the words involuntarily, attempting the accent long unheard. "Au soleil de Messidor, au soleil de Messidor" . . . and his wife and children stared after him as, thrusting the half-eaten bowl aside, he rose and went out, muttering gibberish. They were not unused to these fits in the house-father, to the change in his eyes, the sudden forgetting of their presence; but never lost their fear of them as something uncanny and inexplicable.

With these masterful rushes of the past came often an infinite melancholy; which was not so much a regret for what had been as a sense of the pity of oblivion. So that he would lie outstretched with his face to the earth, rebellious at the thought that with him and a few of his own generation must pass all knowledge of human achievement, the very memory of that which had once been glorious. . . . Not only the memory of actual men whose fame had once been blown about the world; but the memory of sound, of music, and of marvels in stone, uplifted by the skill of generations; the memory of systems, customs, laws, wrought wisely by the hand of experience; and of fanciful people, more real than living men and women. With him and his like would pass not only Leonardo, Cæsar and the sun of Messidor, but Rosalind, d'Artagnan and Faust; the heroes, the merrymen, the women loved and loving who, created of dreams, had shared the dead world with their fellows created of dust. . . . Once deemed immortal, they had been slain by science as surely as their fellows of dust.

At times he pondered vaguely whether he might not save the memory of some of them alive by teaching his children to love them; but in the end he realized that, as we grasp nothing save through ourselves and our own relation to it, the embodied desires and beauty of an inconceivable age would be meaningless to his young barbarians.

If he ceased to believe in the survival of life as he had known it and a civilization that would reach out and claim him, there were times when he believed, or almost believed, that somewhere in the vastness of the great round world a remnant must hold fast to its inheritance; when it was inconceivable that all men living could be sunk in brutishness or vowed to the creed of utter ignorance. Hunger and blind terror—(he knew, for he had seen it)—could reduce the highest to the level of the beast; but with the passing of terror and the satisfaction of the actual needs of the body, there awakens the hunger of the mind. Somewhere in the vastness of the great, round world must be those who, because they craved for more than full stomachs and daily security, still clung to the power which is knowledge. Little groups and companies that chance had brought together or good fortune saved from destruction; resourceful men who had striven with surrounding anarchy and worsted it, and, having worsted it, were building their civilization. . . . And in the very completeness of surrounding anarchy, the very depth of surrounding brutishness, would lie their opportunity and chance of supremacy, their power of enforcing their will.

If such groups, such future nations, existed, he asked himself how they would build? What manner of world they would strive for—knowing what they knew? . . . This, at least, was certain: it would not be the world of their fathers, of their own youth. They had seen their civilization laid waste by the agency of science combined with human passion; hence, if they rejected the alternative of ignorance and held to their perilous treasure of science, their problem was the mastery of passion.

He came to believe that the problem—like all others—had been faced in forgotten generations; that old centuries had learned the forgotten lesson that the Ruin was teaching anew. To a race that had realized the peril of knowledge there would be two alternatives only; renunciation—the creed of blind ignorance and savagery —or the guarding of science as a secret treasure, removed from all contact with the flame that is human emotion. There had been elder and long-past civilizations in which knowledge was a mystery, the possession and the privilege of a caste; tradition had come down to us of ancient

wisdom which might only be revealed to the initiate. . . .
A blind fear massacred its scientific men, a wiser fear
exalted them and set them apart as initiates. When science and human emotion between them had wrought
the extreme of destruction and agony, there passed the
reckless and idealistic dream of a world where all might
be enlightened; the aim and tradition of a social system
arising out of ruin would be the setting of an iron barrier between science and human emotion. That, and not
enlightenment of all and sundry—the admission of the
foolish, the impulsive and the selfish to a share in the
power of destruction. The same need and instinct of self-
preservation which had inspired the taking of the Vow of
Ignorance would work, in higher and saner minds, for
the training of a caste—an Egyptian priesthood—exempt
from blind passion and the common impulse of the herd;
a caste trained in silence and rigid self-control, its way of
attainment made hard to the student, the initiate. The
deadly formulæ of mechanics, electricity and chemistry
would be entrusted only to those who had been purged
of the daily common passions of the multitude; to those
who, by trial after trial, had fettered their natural impulses
and stripped themselves of instinct and desire.

So, in times past, had arisen—and might again arise—
a scientific priesthood whose initiates, to the vulgar, were
magicians; a caste that guarded science as a mystery and
confined the knowledge which is power of destruction to
those who had been trained not to use it. The old lost learning of dead and gone kingdoms was a science shielded by

Theodore Savage

its devotees from defilement by human emotion; a pure, cold knowledge, set apart and worshipped for itself. . . . And somewhere in the vastness of the great round world the beginnings of a priesthood, a scientific caste, might be building unconsciously on the lines of ancient wisdom, and laying the foundations of yet another Egypt or Chaldæa. A State whose growth would be rooted in the mystery of knowledge and fear of human passion; whose culture and civilization would be moulded by a living and terrible tradition of catastrophe through science uncontrolled. . . . And, so long as the tradition was living and terrible, the initiate would stand guard before his mysteries, that the world might be saved from itself; only when humanity had forgotten its downfall and ruin had ceased to be even a legend, would the barrier between science and emotion be withdrawn and knowledge be claimed as the right of the uncontrolled, the multitude.

Till his brain began to fail him he watched, in dumb interest, the life and development of the tribe; learning from it more than he had ever known in the world of his youth of the eternal foundations on which life in community is built. The unending struggle between the desire for freedom, which makes of man a rebel, and the need for security, which makes of him a citizen, was played before his understanding eyes; he watched parties, castes and priesthoods in the making and, before he died, could forecast the beginning of an aristocracy, a slave class and a tribal hereditary monarchy. In all things man untraditioned held blindly to the ways he had forgotten; instinctively, not knowing whither they led, he trod the paths that his fathers had trodden before him.

Most of all he was stirred in his interest and pity by the life religious of the world around him; watching it adapt itself, steadily and naturally, to the needs of a race in its childhood. As a new generation grew up to its heritage of ignorance, the foundations of faith were shifted; as tribal life crystallized, gods multiplied inevitably and the Heaven ruled by a Supreme Being gave place to a crude Valhalla of minor deities. Man, who makes God in his own image, can only make that image in the likeness of his own highest type; which, in a world divided, insecure and predatory, is the type of the successful warrior; the Saviour, in a world divided and predatory, takes the form of a tribal deity who secures to his people the enjoyment of their fields by strengthening their hands against the assaults and the malice of their enemies. As always with those who live in constant fear and in hate of one another, the Lord was a Man of War; and when Theodore's first grandson was received into the tribe, the deity to whom vows were made in the name of the child was already a local Jehovah. Faith saw him as a tribal Lord of Hosts, the celestial captain of his worshippers; if his worshippers walked humbly and paid due honour to his name he would stand before them in the day of battle and protect them with his shield invisible—would draw the sword of the Lord and of Gideon, show himself mightier than the priests of Baal and overthrow the altars of the Philistines.

A god whose attributes are those of a warrior, of necessity is not omnipotent; since he fights, his authority is partial—assailed and disputed by those against whom he draws the sword. A race in its childhood evolved the deity it needed, a champion and upholder of his own people; to the tribal warrior the god to whom an enemy prayed for success was a rival of his own protector. . . . So the mind primitive argued, more or less directly and consciously, making God in its image, for its own needs and purposes; and even in Theodore's lifetime the deities worshipped by men from a distance were not those of his own country. The jurisdiction of the gods was limited and the stranger, of necessity, paid homage to an alien spirit who took pleasure in an unfamiliar ritual.

In his lifetime the darkness of Heaven was unbroken and there emerged no god whose attribute was mercy and long-suffering; the Day of Judgment was still too recent, its memory too clear and overwhelming, to admit of the idea of a Divine Love or a Father who had pity on his children. Fear, and fear only, led his people to the feet of the Lord. The God of Vengeance of the first generation and the tribal superman who gradually ousted him from his pride of place were alike wrathful, jealous of their despotism and greedily expectant of mouth-honour. Hence, propitiation and ignorance were the whole religious duty of man, and the rites wherewith deity was duly worshipped were rites of crawling flattery and sacrifice. . . . The blood of sinners was acceptable in the sight of Heaven; the Lord Almighty had destroyed a world that he might slake his vengeance, and his lineal descendants, the celestial warriors, rejoiced in the slaughter of those who had borne arms against their worshippers—in the end, rejoiced in blood for itself and the savour of the burnt sacrifice. And a race cowed spiritually (lest worse befall it) evolved its rites of sacrificial cruelty, paying tribute to a god who took ceaseless pleasure in the humbling of his people and could only be appeased by their suffering.

There were seasons and regions where abasement produced its own reaction; when, for all the savour of sacrificial cruelty, the gods remained deaf to the prayers of their worshippers, delivered them into the hands of their enemies or chastened them with famine and pestilence. Hope of salvation beaten out of them, the worshippers, like rats driven into a corner, ceased to grovel and turned on the tyrants who had failed them; and the Lord Almighty Who made the heavens, shrunk to the dimensions of a local fetish, was upbraided and beaten in effigy.

Since it seemed that the new world must in all things follow in the ways of the old, the gentler deities who delighted not in blood would in due time reveal themselves to man grown capable of mercy. As the memory of judgment faded with the centuries—as the earth waxed fruitful and life was kindlier—humanity would dare to lift its head from the dust and the life religious would be more than blind cringing to a despot. The Heaven of the future would find room for gods who were gracious and friendly; for white Baldurs and Olympians who walk with men and instruct them; and there would arise prophets whose message was not vengeance, but a call to "rejoice in the Lord." . . . And in further time, it might be, the God who is a Spirit ... and a Christ. ... The rise, the long, slow upward struggle of the soul of man was as destined and inevitable as its fall; all human achievement, material or spiritual, was founded in the baseness of mire and clay—and rose towering above its foundations. As the State, which had its origin in no more than common fear and hatred, in the end would be honoured without thought of gain and its flag held sacred by its sons; so Deity, beginning as vengeance personified, would advance to a spiritual Law and a spiritual Love. When the power of loving returned to the race, it would cease to abase itself and lift up its eyes to a Father—endowing its Deity with that which was best in itself; when it achieved and took pleasure in its own thoughts and the works of its hands, it would see in the Highest not the Vengeance that destroys but the Spirit that heals and creates.

Meanwhile the foundation of the life religious was, and must be, the timorous virtue of ignorance, of humble avoidance of inquiry into the dreadful secrets of God. In Theodore's youth he had turned from the orthodox religions, which repelled by what seemed to him a fear of knowledge and inquiry; now he understood that man, being by nature destructive, can survive only when his powers of destruction are limited; and that the ignorance enjoined by priest and bigot had been—and would be again—an essential need of the race, an expression of the will to live. ... The jealous God who guards his secrets is the god of the race that survives.

How many times—(he would wonder)—how many times since the world began to spin has man, in his eager search for truth, rushed blindly through knowledge to the ruin that means chaos and savagery? How many times, in his devout, instinctive longing to know his own nature and the workings of the Infinite Mind that created him has he wrought himself weapons that turned to his own destruction? . . . Ignorance of the powers and forces of nature is a condition of human existence; as necessary to the continued life of the race as the breathing of air or the taking of food into the body. Behind the bench of zealots who judged Galileo lay the dumb race-memory of ruin—ruin, perhaps, many times repeated. They stood, the zealots, for that ignorance which, being interpreted, is life; and Galileo for that knowledge which, being interpreted, is death. . . .

Many times, it might be, since the world began to spin, had men called upon the rocks to cover them from the devils their own hands had fashioned; many times, it might be, a remnant had put from it the knowledge it dared not trust itself to wield—that it might not fall upon its own weapons, but live, just live, like the beasts! Behind the injunction to devout ignorance, behind the ecclesiastical hatred of science and distrust of brain, lay more than prejudice and bigotry; the prejudice and bigotry were but superficial and outward workings of instinct and the first law of all, the Law of Self-Preservation.

With his eyes open to the workings of that law, folktale and myth had long become real to him—since he saw them daily in the making. . . . The dragon that wasted a country with its breath—how else should a race that knew naught of chemistry account for the devilry of gas?

And he understood now, why the legend of Icarus was a legend of disaster, and Prometheus, who stole fire from Heaven, was chained to eternity for his daring; he knew, also, why the angel with a flaming sword barred the gate of Eden to those who had tasted of knowledge. . . . The story of the Garden, of the Fall of Man, was no more the legend of his youth; he read it now, with his opened eyes, as a livid and absolute fact. A fact told plainly as symbol could tell it by a race that had put from it all memory of the science whereby it was driven from its ancient paradise, its garden of civilization. . . . How many times since the world began to spin had man mastered the knowledge that should make him like unto God, and turned, in agony of mind and body, from a power synonymous with death?

And how many times more, he wondered—how many times more?

Theodore Savage lived to be a very old man; how old in years he could not have said, since, long before his memory failed him, he had lost his count of time. But for fully a decade before he died he went humped and rheumatic, leaning on a stick, was blear-eyed, toothless and wizened; he had outlived all those who had begun the new world with him, and a son of his grandson was of those who—when the time came—dug a trench for his bones and shovelled loose earth on his head.

He had no lack of care in his extreme old age—in part perhaps because the tribe grew to hold him in awe that increased with the years; the sole survivor of the legendary age that preceded the Ruin and Downfall of Man, he was feared in spite of his helplessness. He alone of his little community could remember the Ruin with any comprehension of its causes; he alone possessed in silence a share of that hidden and forbidden knowledge which had brought flaming judgment on the world. Here and there in the countryside were grey-headed men, his juniors by years, who could remember vaguely the horrors of a distant childhood—the sky afire, the crash of falling masonry, the panic, the lurking and the starving. These things they could remember like a nightmare past . . . but only remember, not explain. Behind Theodore's bald forehead and dimmed, oozing eyes lay the understanding of why and wherefore denied to those who dwelt beside him.

For this reason Theodore Savage was treated with deference in the days of his senile helplessness. As he sat, half-blind, in the sun by the door of his hut, no one ever failed to greet him with respect in passing; while in most the greeting was more than a token of respect or kindliness—the sign and result of a nervous desire to propitiate. In the end he was credited with a knowledge of unholy arts, and the children of the tribe avoided and shrank from him, frightened by the gossip of their elders; so that village mothers found him useful as a bogy, arresting the tantrums of unruly brats by threats of calling in Old Bald-Head.

Even in his lifetime legends clustered thick about him, and sickness or accident to man or beast was ascribed to the glance of his purblind eye or the malice of his vacant brain; while there was once—though he never knew or suspected it—an agitated and furtive discussion as to whether, for the good of the community, he should not be knocked on the head. The furtive discussion ended in discussion only—not because the advocates of mercy were numerous, but because no man was willing to lay violent hands on a wizard, for fear of what might befall him; and, the interlude over, the tribe relapsed into its customary timid respect for its patriarch, its customary practice of ensuring his goodwill by politeness and small offerings of victuals. These added to the old man's comfort in his latter years—nor had he any suspicion of the motive that secured him both deference and dainties.

With his death the local legends increased and multiplied; the distorted, varied myths of the Ruin of Man and its causes showing an inevitable tendency to group themselves around one striking and mysterious figure, to make of that figure a cause and a personification of the Great Disaster. Theodore Savage, to those who came after, was Merlin, Frankenstein and Adam; the fool who tasted of forbidden fruit, the magician whose arts had brought ruin on a world, the devil-artisan whose unholy skill had created monsters that destroyed him. His grave was an awesome spot, apart from other graves, which the timorous avoided after dark; and, long after all trace of it had vanished, there clung to the neighbourhood a tradition of haunting and mystery. . . . To his children's children his name was the symbol of a dead civilization; a civilization that had passed so completely from the ken of living man that its lost achievements, the manner of its ending, could only be expressed in symbol.

Cicely Hamilton (1872–1952) was an Anglo-Irish actress, author, and feminist campaigner best known for her 1909 treatise *Marriage as a Trade*. Her prewar plays include *Diana of Dobson's* (1908) and *How the Vote Was Won* (1909). After working in the north of France during WWI and witnessing how its violence affected civilians, she was inspired to write *Theodore Savage* (1922), a proto-sf novel presciently foregrounding modern warfare's destructive power.

Susan R. Grayzel is Professor of History at Utah State University, where she researches and teaches about modern European history, women's and gender history, the history of the world wars, and war and culture. Her publications in these areas include *Women's Identities at War* (1999) and *At Home and Under Fire: Air Raids and Culture in Britain from the Great War to the Blitz* (2012). Her latest book is *The Age of the Gas Mask: How British Civilians Faced the Terrors of Total War* (Cambridge University Press, 2022).